"Why is this happening?"

Jeff touched Lindsey's shoulder. "Get some rest. Ray will run me home, then he'll be out here till you're ready to go. I'll relieve him and take you to the restaurant. You shouldn't walk–"

"You really don't have to–"

"Lindsey." He interrupted her, then paused and let out a slow breath. "I know I didn't take care of you tonight–"

Without thinking, she cupped his cheek with her free hand, stopping his words. "You did all anyone could do." The doubt in his eyes made Lindsey ache in a way she didn't quite understand, but she knew neither of them could deal with it tonight. Slowly she eased her hand away. "I'll see you at four." Straightening and pulling open the screen door, Lindsey unlocked her home and reached in to turn on the light.

Then she screamed.

D0180957

Books by Ramona Richards

Love Inspired Suspense

A Murder Among Friends
The Face of Deceit
The Taking of Carly Bradford
Field of Danger
House of Secrets
Memory of Murder

RAMONA RICHARDS

A writer and editor since 1975, Ramona Richards has worked on staff with a number of publishers. Ramona has also freelanced with more than twenty magazine and book publishers and has won awards for both her fiction and nonfiction. She's written everything from sales-training video scripts to book reviews, and her latest articles have appeared in *Today's Christian Woman, College Bound* and *Special Ed Today.* She sold a story about her daughter to *Chicken Soup for the Caregiver's Soul,* and *Secrets of Confidence,* a book of devotionals, is available from Barbour Publishing.

In 2004 the God Allows U-Turns Foundation, in conjunction with the Advanced Writers and Speakers Association (AWSA), chose Ramona for their "Strength of Choice" award, and in 2003 AWSA nominated Ramona for Best Fiction Editor of the Year. The Evangelical Press Association presented her with an award for reporting in 2003, and in 1989 she won the Bronze Award for Best Original Dramatic Screenplay at the Houston International Film Festival. A member of the American Christian Fiction Writers and the Romance Writers of America, she has five other novels complete or in development.

MEMORY OF MURDER

RAMONA RICHARDS

HARLEQUIN® LOVE INSPIRED® SUSPENSE

If you purchased this book without a cover you should be aware that this book is stolen property. It was reported as "unsold and destroyed" to the publisher, and neither the author nor the publisher has received any payment for this "stripped book."

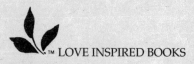

Recycling programs for this product may not exist in your area.

™ LOVE INSPIRED BOOKS

ISBN-13: 978-0-373-67552-4

MEMORY OF MURDER

Copyright © 2013 by Ramona Richards

All rights reserved. Except for use in any review, the reproduction or utilization of this work in whole or in part in any form by any electronic, mechanical or other means, now known or hereafter invented, including xerography, photocopying and recording, or in any information storage or retrieval system, is forbidden without the written permission of the editorial office, Love Inspired Books, 233 Broadway, New York, NY 10279 U.S.A.

This is a work of fiction. Names, characters, places and incidents are either the product of the author's imagination or are used fictitiously, and any resemblance to actual persons, living or dead, business establishments, events or locales is entirely coincidental.

This edition published by arrangement with Love Inspired Books.

® and TM are trademarks of Love Inspired Books, used under license. Trademarks indicated with ® are registered in the United States Patent and Trademark Office, the Canadian Trade Marks Office and in other countries.

www.LoveInspiredBooks.com

Printed in U.S.A.

He that dwelleth in the secret place of the most High
shall abide under the shadow of the Almighty.
I will say of the Lord, he is my refuge and my
fortress: my God; in him will I trust. Surely he shall
deliver thee from the snare of the fowler, and from
the noisome pestilence. He shall cover thee with
his feathers, and under his wings shalt thou trust:
his truth shall be thy shield and buckler.
Thou shalt not be afraid for the terror by night;
nor for the arrow that flieth by day.
—*Psalms* 91:1–5

To Sharon, who has learned to live Psalm 91:5,
growing stronger every day.

ONE

Her every nerve suddenly on edge, Lindsey Presley stared at the blond man confronting Deputy Jeff Gage.

Reaching behind her, Lindsey double-checked the lock on the front door of her restaurant, then hugged the night-deposit bag more tightly. She prayed she was wrong about the stranger. After all, he didn't look all that different from other young people in the area. Clean-shaven, short hair, T-shirt, jeans. Barely more than a kid. Average.

Except for that vintage orange 1968 Pontiac GTO that waited behind him, blocking Jeff's patrol cruiser. The GTO's front door stood open, waiting. Its motor idled with the distinctive rumble of a pampered muscle car.

The top step of the Cape Cod–style building gave Lindsey a view of the entire parking lot. Empty, except for the three of them and the two cars. She blinked hard, distracted as the kid shook his left hand out to one side, as if trying to fling a bug from it. His right hand remained hidden behind his hip.

Go back inside. This isn't right. A streetwise instinct honed in her childhood urged Lindsey to flee behind closed doors. There a kitchen bristled with knives she could use for defense. But that instinct fought with her reluctance to leave the sheriff's deputy who stood between her and the young man. Jeff had promised to protect her on the nightly deposit runs to the bank and had done just that since she'd opened the diner six months ago. During those short rides to the bank, they'd become close friends. She didn't want to abandon him. She wouldn't.

Friends don't do that. And the guy still hasn't done anything wrong. Logic told her to wait. Friendship begged her to stay. Her gut told her to run.

Jeff, who had been waiting for her at the foot of the front steps at eight o'clock, also seemed to sense something odd about the way the young man had slid the GTO into the parking lot after closing time. He stood with his back stiff, feet apart and firmly planted, his hand on his gun. On guard and wary.

The man's left hand shook harder, and Lindsey's muscles tensed. Now, she thought. It's going to happen now. What do I do?

Trip the alarm. The thought startled her, but she immediately knew it was a good idea. Turning, she thrust her key in the lock, twisted it and cracked open the door. If she didn't close it or enter the code inside within thirty seconds, the alarm would sound.

"Sir, you need to leave." Jeff's firm command echoed over the empty parking lot. "The restaurant is closed."

Lindsey pivoted back toward the parking lot, eyes fixed on the two men. The younger man shook his head, now holding his left hand high and smiling broadly. "I understand. I understand. I just need directions. I drove all the way from... from Chicago. Trying to find a girl I met online. Just a girl." He stepped forward, as if to go around Jeff.

Jeff blocked his path. He glanced warily up at the kid's left hand. "Where are you going?"

The blond never responded. Instead, he swung his right arm around from behind his back. He ground a stun gun into Jeff's chest. With a stark cry of pain, Jeff dropped to the asphalt, his body twisting in spastic seizures.

"No!" Lindsey screamed. She dashed down

the steps toward them, throwing the money bag at the man. "Take it!" She lunged toward Jeff.

She never reached him. Fire shot through her skull as the man grabbed her by the hair, yanking her backward. He punched her in the solar plexus. Lindsey's breath stopped and spots danced in front of her eyes as she collapsed. Her assailant grabbed her arm and slung her over the hood of the GTO.

The restaurant alarm blared through the night, the sirens radiating off every wall in the neighborhood. The man cursed and pressed his arm on the back of her neck. "Stupid woman!"

Lindsey fought for air as he yanked her arms behind her. Plastic ties cut deep into her skin as he secured her wrists. Finally drawing a raspy gasp, Lindsey tried to scream again, but a sharp blow to her ribs cut it off as she curled up in agony. He snapped her ankles together, wrapping the ties around them. He tossed her over one shoulder, her small frame no burden at all to him.

He bent to scoop up the money, then kicked Jeff twice as he passed the struggling deputy— once in the side, once on the back of Jeff's skull. Jeff went limp.

Lindsey found more breath. "No!" She bucked against the man, but he ignored her, shoving her unceremoniously into the backseat of the GTO.

"Scream away, darlin'. No one will hear you over this baby."

The guy got in and gunned the engine. The fine-tuned rumble exploded into a roar that split the night air. The orange car spit loose gravel, and smoke bellowed from beneath its tires as it spun out of the parking lot less than five minutes after it had pulled in.

Lindsey pushed herself around, still fighting to breathe normally, regularly. Not an easy task with the pain throbbing through her ribs and head. She struggled against her bonds without success. Sweat coated her back and legs where they pressed against the vinyl backseat of the car. The fury and adrenaline that seared through her made Lindsey's mind spin. Her muscles trembled, but terror and pain kept her sane and focused as the past few minutes played over and over in her head.

God, how do I get out of this? Help me.

Lindsey twisted until she could see her attacker over the low, split front seat of the GTO. His pasty face glowed in the glare of oncoming headlights, and rivulets of water dripped out of the man's hair and trailed down his cheeks and neck.

He's sweating! Despite the open front windows and light chill of the early fall night, the man's hair remained plastered to his scalp. He fidgeted, drumming his fingers on the steering wheel and squirming in his seat. He pulled a slip of paper from his shirt pocket to check it, mumbling directions to himself. Over the roar of the engine, Lindsey barely caught the words, "Go slow. Careful. Left after three miles." He shoved the paper back in his pocket. He let up on the gas, and the car slowed.

He's going to turn. Leave the main road. Lindsey knew the road he planned to take. It ran deep into an almost impenetrable Tennessee woodland. In that second's realization, Lindsey knew she was about to die. *No!* Her mind screamed the word, and in pure desperation, a rough idea formed in her mind. An insane idea. *He'll be focused on the turn, the other cars...*

As Lindsey slowly shifted her body into position, her assailant's words repeated over and over.

Turn, three miles. Turn, three miles.

Lindsey frowned, then blinked the words away. She must get ready, no matter how crazy her plan seemed. *You can do this. You can do this!* Pushing over on her back, she ignored the agony in her hands as she braced her shoulders against the middle of the seat and cautiously drew her knees up to her chest. Her short, petite frame let her curl into a tight ball, and Lindsey had never felt so grateful for being so short—or for taking that Pilates class her sisters had insisted on.

Still mumbling, the man braked the car suddenly, shouting at an oncoming vehicle to get out of the way. As he stomped on the accelerator again, heading the car into the left turn, Lindsey shrieked with all her might. Startled, the man's head snapped around to glare at her, just as she kicked both legs with as much strength as she had, thrusting her thick-soled, restaurant-durable shoes directly at his face.

His scream matched hers as blood shot from his crushed nose. He jerked, twisting the wheel to the right, veering the car out of the turn and straight toward the corner where the two roads met. He never had a chance to touch the brakes as the orange GTO crashed through the guardrail and soared into the air. The engine howled as the tires left the road. Lindsey felt weightless, her body floating above the seat as the car arced into the ravine. Then the car plowed into the rock and dirt, landing grill down with a deafening sound of sheared metal and shattering glass.

Lindsey plunged forward over the seat. Searing pain sliced through her as her shins hit the man's head, which slammed forward into the steering wheel with a sickening crack. She crashed into the windshield, then down on the dash as the car rolled over on its right side. It slid another few yards before the weight of the engine pulled it upright again.

Lindsey's head thudded into the dash a second time, and the darkness of unconsciousness consumed her.

Jeff groaned as consciousness returned. Rocks and dirt bit into his cheek, and he tried to raise his head, which throbbed with a deep, unrelenting pain. *Lindsey! Oh, dear God, what did he do to Lindsey?* The silent air around him deepened his sense of panic. *What happened to the alarm?*

He heard the crunch of hard soles on gravel and tried to push up, only to have a foot land in the middle of his back, shoving him back to the ground. With quick, efficient moves, the man plucked Jeff's handcuffs off his belt and secured the deputy's hands behind him.

"Relax, boy. She'll be dead before you can get to your feet."

Jeff clawed through his memory, trying to recognize the rough voice, but nothing registered. His brain felt as fried as his muscles.

But Lindsey couldn't be dead. She couldn't. An agony laced through Jeff's chest that had nothing to do with his physical injuries. "No." His voice croaked.

The man bent closer but deftly stayed out of Jeff's line of sight. "Oh, yes. You're worthless, boy. If that woman were still alive, she'd hate you for abandoning her. Sheriff Taylor should fire you. And he will by the time we get through with you. We'll be watching and waiting for the next chance to make you fail."

Jeff spit gravel out of his mouth and tried to speak. Then he heard the ominous buzz just before the spears of pain hit his shoulder. Lightning shots of current sheared through him again, and Jeff screamed in rage and despair.

Nothing smells like a wrecked car. Lindsey had been in more than one accident, and the smells always lingered in her memory. Hot oil, burnt rubber, gasoline and stressed metal. Acrid smoke burned her nose. It had startled Lindsey to consciousness, but now she just wanted to get away from it. She tried to move, but her shoulders felt wedged beneath the dash. A low moan escaped her as each and every inch of her body felt battered and bruised.

It was an old feeling, deep from within her childhood, and she pushed it away, mentally going over her body to survey her injuries. The coppery taste in her mouth and swollen cheek and lips meant a blow to the face, and the slick and sticky liquid coating her hands told her that the plastic ties had cut deep into her skin. Her right shoulder felt twisted. One ankle throbbed with a terrible ache, but nothing felt broken. Her father had dealt her far worse.

While her injuries were excruciating, Lindsey was even more terrified that she stared, face-to-face, at her attacker. Her small, limp frame had crumpled and wedged itself in the passenger floorboard. Unbelted, the man had toppled from behind the wheel when the car went up on its right side. He'd smashed headfirst into the passenger-side window, then slid down in the seat as the car settled back on four wheels. Even unconscious and bleeding from two major head wounds, he felt menacing. Though frightened, Lindsey forced herself to remain still.

Who are *you?* Ghostly pale, his round face still had a babyish quality to it, like that of a teenager. She'd never seen him before, and from Jeff's reaction back at the restaurant, he hadn't recognized the attacker, either. And Lindsey felt pretty certain that Deputy Jeff Gage knew just about everyone in Bell County.

Jeff. Her thoughts flashed back to the restaurant, to the sight of Jeff lying motionless on the ground. "Please, Lord," she whispered. "Let him be okay." In that moment, Lindsey realized she really wanted Jeff here, to see him, to know he was all right. For him to tell her everything would be all right.

"Please. Get us out of this."

Out. I have to get out. Lindsey tried to move, to straighten her legs, but she almost screamed from the pain that shot through her muscles and joints. She gave up, taking comfort in the sound of someone scrambling around in the brush outside the car.

"We're here!" she called out. "Please help us!"

A blinding light hit her face, and Lindsey grimaced, trying to turn away. "Hey!"

"You're supposed to be dead. Again."

Lindsey stilled. "Who are you?"

A gloved hand reached in through the passenger window and fumbled around the body of her unconscious assailant. "Is he dead?"

Fear seized Lindsey now, freezing her tongue. An old memory shot through her, one from her childhood. A voice that had made her stop in her tracks, unable to speak. Words so similar, Lindsey wondered if she were hallucinating. *You're supposed to be dead. Is she dead?*

She. Not *he.* Lindsey blinked hard, trying to clear the fog in her mind. Everything felt mixed up, the past and present running together like paint colors. *Why can't I remember!*

"No matter." The hand kept pulling at the man's clothes until it found the shirt pocket. "If he's not, he will be soon. Stupid...deserves to die for wrecking this car. What a waste. Beautiful machine." Fingers clawed into the pocket, plucking the piece of paper from it. "And for not completing his job with you."

The street-savvy kid who still lived deep inside Lindsey reacted instinctively, and she twisted hard, shoving herself deeper beneath the dash. She screamed just as the light swung in her direction, smashing into the spot where her head had been. The light shattered and went out. The man cursed, condemning her and everything on the planet. He reached through the window and clawed desperately at the glove compartment, but wasn't able to get it open.

Sirens split the night air, and the sound of urgent voices echoed into the ravine. The man cursed again, backing away from the car. "We're not done with you. We're around every corner."

As he crashed away through the brush, Lindsey sobbed.

Another light pierced the car, and Lindsey screamed, terror shooting through her.

"Lindsey! It's okay. We're here to help." This

time the warm, soothing tones belonged to Sheriff Ray Taylor, and relief flooded through her as she recognized the baritone voice of her brother-in-law.

"Ray! Please get me out of here."

"As soon as we can, hon. Hang in there with me."

Lindsey closed her eyes, let out a slow, ragged breath and nodded.

"Jeff. Talk to me, son."

Jeff heard the voice, but consciousness did not return easily, no matter how hard he tried. Light hurt. Sound hurt.

Everything hurt.

"Jeff, can you hear me?"

Jeff Gage recognized the gentle but gravelly voice of the EMT. Alan Gage. His stepfather. Other voices hovered over him. Alan's fellow EMTs and other deputies. Firm hands helped ease him onto a backboard, and a cervical collar stabilized his head.

"Lindsey." Jeff's voice still sounded as if he'd swallowed a load of mulch. He tried to open his eyes, but the light burned them, making more pain spear into his skull. The odor of a strong antiseptic blended with the smell of gravel dust. Jeff fought the urge to sneeze.

Alan squeezed his arm. "I know. They found her. Ray's with her now."

"She all right?"

Alan hesitated, and Jeff's gut knotted. He twisted, testing his muscles against the belts of the gurney as it rolled toward the ambulance. "Alan, I don't need this. Let me up."

The grizzled EMT made a sound that was somewhere between a snort and a growl. He placed an arm over Jeff's chest. "Boy, you ain't goin' nowhere. That car Lindsey was in crashed. She's awake and headed for the hospital. So are you. You have a knot on the back of your head the size of a grapefruit. You've been hit with two full doses of a stun gun, so you got a nice burn on your chest and one on your shoulder. Thrashing around on the ground scraped you up pretty good, and it looks like you took a shot to the ribs as well as to your skull. Maybe a couple of breaks. Maybe a concussion. We'll let the docs sort it out. You ain't going nowhere but the hospital, and your mother would kill me if I even let you try."

Jeff stared up at Alan, his words like acid in his throat. "I should have protected her. I failed her." He grimaced. "They're coming after us again."

"Hold still, Lindsey. I'm going to cut the ties." Behind her back, there was a soft snip, and her hands fell free, releasing her shoulders and arms from their painful and stretched position. They couldn't get her out of the mangled car, but she'd managed to twist so that Ray could cut the plastic ties. She sighed with relief. "How's Jeff?"

Sheriff Ray Taylor's mouth twitched, as if he were fighting his true thoughts. Instead, he cleared his throat, his baritone voice as gruff as his words. "He's at the hospital. Which is where you're going." He snapped his pocketknife closed, then draped a heavy, protective blanket over Lindsey as, behind him, two rescue workers pushed their way through the brush and debris with the Jaws of Life.

Ray had not left her since he'd scrambled down to the car, shoving aside anything in his way. Still hyped on adrenaline and fear, she'd babbled out everything that had happened. He took in every word calmly. When she got to the part about the man with the flashlight, he'd turned and said something to an officer behind him, then faced her again.

For the first time, Lindsey saw Ray in action as a sheriff, not just as her brother-in-law. He insisted that she focus on him instead of the unconscious assailant still trapped in the car with her—to keep her awake and alert. Although Lindsey knew all the reasons her sister June had fallen for the easygoing sheriff, she now saw why Jeff admired his mentor and boss. She saw in Ray the same mannerisms that she'd noticed so often in Jeff.

Ray moved aside to allow the EMTs to reach her. One of the rescue workers peered in, evaluating the situation. "I'm going to cover you both. Then we're going to cut into the roof as well as get this door open. It's going to be really loud, and the whole car will vibrate. When we get access, everything will happen fast. We'll grab him first, then you. You holler if any shifts cause your pain to get worse."

Lindsey nodded, and he pulled the blanket over both of them, tucking it in tight. In the abrupt darkness, Lindsey let out another ragged sigh and closed her eyes. Tears ran down her cheeks again, and she pushed away thoughts of how close the man who had tried to kidnap her was to her face, that he could wake up at any moment. Even with the workers outside and the sheriff close, Lindsey's fear of the man hovered near. He'd acted and sounded so crazy!

Outside the car, a sputtering engine roared to full power, like a chain saw on steroids. The car rocked with the first effort, and Lindsey squeezed her eyes tighter as pain shot through her hips and back. Nothing she couldn't handle.

Again her mind snapped to her childhood and the abuse her father had inflicted.

The shriek of ripping metal helped Lindsey push the memory away, and she gritted her teeth against the sound. Then voices called, echoing around the ravine with a new fervor. Someone peeled the blanket away, and Lindsey blinked as light and cooler air flooded in. Two men reached in, gently easing her attacker onto a backboard. Over the cacophony of the rescue efforts, she heard the steady whup-whup of a helicopter.

"Lifeflight?" she asked one of the EMTs.

He nodded. "They're taking him to Vanderbilt. You'll probably go to NorthCrest, unless you're hurt worse than we think."

"Bruises, cuts, some pulled muscles. And I think I twisted my ankle when it hit the dash. Nothing major."

Finalizing his work on the attacker, the EMT nodded at his coworkers and the backboard disappeared as it moved up the side of the ravine. He turned his attention to Lindsey. "You a nurse?"

"No. But I've been hurt bad before. I know how it feels."

He reached in and slid a foam cervical collar around her neck. "How 'bout we let the docs decide?"

Lindsey took a deep breath. "Just didn't want you fussing over me without reason."

The EMT grinned at her. "My job. Now I'm going to see if I can slide this board between you and the seat. You ready?"

"My sisters will tell you I'm always ready for the next step."

"I can believe that. Now, don't move. Don't try to help me. Let me do the work."

Lindsey closed her eyes again, fighting the urge to claw her own way out of this stupid car.

No. Not just a car. A 1968 GTO. A *bright orange* 1968 GTO. The image of her father, his face battered and blotted, shot through her mind again, along with another shadowy figure. Entwined with them was the image of the orange GTO. Lindsey gasped. Why did that happen? What could her father have to do with the car? More importantly…

"Is she dead?"

What am I remembering? And why?

TWO

"Mild concussion. Ribs bruised but fortunately not broken. Cuts and abrasions, along with the burn, which—"

"In other words, I can get back to work. Now." Jeff tugged his uniform shirt closed and buttoned it, trying to ignore the dirt smears and tiny tears from the gravel. He tucked it into his waistband, wincing at the soreness in his chest and muscles. The bandages they'd taped over his few injuries pulled against his skin as he tightened his belt.

Nick Collins, the emergency-room doctor who had treated more than his fair share of the sheriff's officers, stopped typing on a mini-laptop and looked up at Jeff over the top of his reading glasses. "What's got you in such a snit? You're usually the calm one on Ray's team."

Standing behind Nick, Sheriff Ray Taylor spoke grimly. "He failed in his duty."

Jeff scowled, feeling his face heat up, as Nick took off the black-framed glasses and tucked them into the pocket of his white coat. "Well, you also got kicked in the head. That sounds more amusing than it is. I don't want you taking chances with that. Besides, the guy who did it is in a coma at Vanderbilt and Lindsey is a few rooms over, giving our nurses a run for their money. She'll be all right. What's left to do tonight?"

Ray shifted his weight but before he could reply, Jeff snapped, "Forensics. I want to look in the car. And review the reports, and talk to Lindsey about—"

Nick closed the mini-laptop and moved toward Jeff. "Now slow down. I get the picture. I don't want to take any chances on the concussion. I've said you can leave, but only if there's someone who can check on you tonight and in the morning."

Jeff grabbed the opening. "I live over my parents' garage."

"Your dad is Alan Gage, right?"

Jeff nodded. "Stepdad."

"Whatever. If Alan will agree to check in on you, I'll have you out of here in an hour." Nick nodded once, then turned and pushed through the door of Jeff's E.R. room.

Ray stepped up in his place, speaking before Jeff could get a word out. "No. Absolutely not."

"Ray—"

"No." The sheriff crossed his arms over his chest. "First, you were on duty, but you were also a victim. I'll have to think twice about your level of involvement. Second, Troy and his tow truck are at the scene. He's going to haul the GTO to the garage, and we'll go over it tomorrow. No one's going to touch it."

"His garage isn't secure enough for a kidnap—"

"It'll be fine. Troy's Rottweilers won't let anyone touch it."

"But—"

Ray put up a palm. "Jeff, quit pushing. You keep this up, and I'll ask Nick to keep you overnight. Be satisfied that they're dismissing you and that Lindsey's not hurt any worse than she is."

Jeff let out a long breath as the door opened behind Ray. "No thanks to me."

Ray stepped closer. "You did nothing wrong. No one could have thrown off two attacks like that."

"That boy raised a lot of red flags. I should have paid attention."

"Stop that!" A small hand waved at him, and Lindsey limped into the room, a crutch under one arm. "You did everything you could."

Jeff's eyes widened at the sight of her. "Everything but stop him."

Ray scowled. "Both of you hush. Lindsey, what are you doing out of bed?"

Lindsey forced a small smile made crooked by her swollen jaw. A sharp feeling spiked right into Jeff's chest. "I refuse."

Both men stared at her. "What?" Jeff asked.

Lindsey looked at him. "It's our rallying cry. The Presley sisters." She glanced at Ray. "You can ask June about it. She wrote it. Made us memorize it. We'd say it to each other when things with our dad turned horrible. 'I refuse to give up, give in, give over. I refuse to be defeated. He won't win.' After a while, we'd just look at each other and say 'I refuse.'"

She turned back to Jeff. "I know what the second guy did, what he threatened. To both of us. Yeah, he nearly scared me to death. But I refuse. And Ray's right. I'm fine."

"You don't look fine."

Ray muttered, "Oh, boy," as Lindsey's blue eyes widened.

She pushed a loose strand of blond hair behind her ear and stood a little taller. "I beg your pardon."

Jeff felt the heat rising in his cheeks again.

"That's *not* what I meant! You look great. Always. But you're hurt. I mean—the bandages—"

Lindsey nodded. "And the cuts and bruises."

"Yeah..."

"And the limp. I twisted my ankle. Not bad. Just a mild sprain."

"Yes..."

"They'll heal. I really will be all right."

Jeff shook his head. "Lindsey, that's not all—"

"And the guy who did it is in a coma."

"But he didn't do it alone."

A rigid silence hung in the air a few moments, then Ray spoke quietly. "So let's go over it again."

Jeff sat up straighter, wincing a bit from the pain of his bruised ribs. Ray took more notes as Jeff repeated his version of the night's events. "I can't get this out of my mind. The first guy was a kid. Not more than twenty, if that. And really strung out on something. Meth. Coke. Something."

Lindsey nodded again, watching Jeff closely. "He was sweating like a pig. Muttering. Totally stressed out."

"And that car." He looked at Ray. "You know what a classic GTO in prime condition is worth?"

"About fifty grand, last time I checked."

"So would it be your first choice for a kidnapping? Why not a van or an SUV? Something more practical. Nondescript. Cheap."

"You think it was stolen or that it belonged to the second guy?"

Jeff shrugged. "I don't know. But I do think the second guy was in charge. The kid was a mess, but the second guy...he was cold, unfeeling. The kid used the stun gun on me because he had to. The older guy did it because he *wanted* to."

"Turn, three miles."

Both men looked at Lindsey. "What?" asked Jeff.

She watched him closely, curiosity lighting her eyes. "That's what the kid kept repeating. 'Turn, three miles.' And..." She took a deep breath. "He didn't know where he was going."

Ray and Jeff exchanged looks. "How do you know?" asked Ray.

"He had directions written down on paper. Kept checking them, talking to himself. That's how I knew he was about to turn left. How I knew when to try something. And that paper is what the other guy stole out of the car."

Ray focused on Jeff again. "Well, Deputy Gage, looks like you have a lot of work to do on this one."

Jeff stared at his boss. "You're letting me take the lead on this?"

"Watching you two, I'm not sure I could stop you. Both of your minds are already clicking through the steps. But you do everything by the book. Document everything. No shortcuts that could undermine our case in court. Understood?"

"Yes, sir."

"Now, I'll get you and Lindsey home, and keep the guard on her tonight. I'll bring her back to the station in the morning. Meet us there first thing, and we'll get her statement and get the investigation up and running."

"I have to open for breakfast at five-thirty."

Jeff stared at Lindsey, her words sinking in. "You're opening the restaurant tomorrow?"

Lindsey nodded, her eyes wide. "Of course, I am. The restaurant has only been open six months. The commuters have gotten into the routine of stopping for my coffee before work, and I'm getting a crew of regulars who come in for breakfast. People are *expecting* me to be there. I can't close when I'm perfectly capable of opening. That would be ridiculous."

"Lindsey, you are still in danger. What if he comes back to the restaurant and you're hurt worse?" Jeff couldn't keep the desperation out of his voice. He never wanted to see her hurt again.

"Do you really think someone would try again with a restaurant full of people?"

"The point is we don't know what will happen."

"Well, I'm not about to put my job on hold while you do yours."

"Lindsey—"

"No."

Jeff sighed. "Why is that everyone's favorite word tonight?" He looked at Ray, whose mouth twisted into a smirk. "What are you smiling at?"

"Just thinking about how many times I've had a similar debate with my wife." He looked at Lindsey. "If I didn't know you were sisters, I would know you were sisters." Ray's wife, June, notorious for her quick temper and outspoken nature, had stood her ground against Ray and Jeff numerous times.

After a few moments of silent impasse, Ray cleared his throat. "Lindsey, let's compromise. We'll go to the station tonight and get your statement. Then Jeff and I can pick up the investigation in the morning while you make breakfast. Will you agree to having a patrol cruiser in your lot?"

She grinned. "Sure. Cops always know the best places to eat. It'll be good for business."

After a trauma, many people had trouble even remembering their own names. Not Lindsey. Jeff listened as she gave her statement, amazed at her clarity of memory and succinct descriptions of the evening's horrifying events. As for himself, he could recall less now than earlier, and he remembered little of what happened after being stunned the first time. But even struggling to stave off exhaustion and the effects of the painkillers, he replayed the incident in his own mind as she talked, deconstructing every moment, every move. *What could I have done differently?*

His sense of failure knifed into his chest with a pain sharper than the blow to his ribs. He'd not only fallen short as a deputy but as a man. When Ray had asked for volunteers for the nightly escort—obviously a favor for his wife—Jeff had readily stepped up. He hadn't dated since his mother's bout with breast cancer two years earlier, and when he'd met Lindsey at Ray and June's wedding, Jeff had been immediately attracted by her charm, intelligence and determination to make a success of her dream to open a restaurant.

And a little intimidated by that determination as well as her aloofness…until he realized that she worked hard to keep everyone at arm's length—not just him. Even her own sisters didn't know her well. When they both discovered he could make her laugh, a part of the shell fell away. They'd finally become close friends, and he'd hoped it would go further, but now…he'd failed her.

Lindsey glanced at him as she finished her official description of the car and her assailant.

He nodded his agreement; what she said matched what he remembered.

Lindsey paused, her eyes narrowing as she studied him closer. "Are you all right?"

Jeff sat up straighter, rolling his shoulders back. "Sure. The painkillers are taking full effect, but I'm all right. Go on."

Ray glanced at him, as well, then turned as Lindsey resumed her statement. For the first time, Jeff truly absorbed what had happened to her, how she'd caused the accident. Her strength astonished him. "You took an awful chance."

She crossed her arms over her chest. "I learned a long time ago that getting hurt is better than dying."

Jeff's eyebrows arched up, but he didn't respond. Instead, he focused on every move she made as she finished. Every eye shift, muscle twitch. She looked at the digital recorder in front of Ray, occasionally glancing up at the sheriff. Lindsey's expressions smoothed out as she talked, and she became almost motionless.

In truth, this was the first time in the six months of their friendship that Jeff had been able to study Lindsey so closely. During their nightly rides, he mostly focused on the road as they headed from the diner to the bank, then to the small cottage Lindsey had rented. She had chosen a sweet but unadorned rental within walking distance of the restaurant. She told him the morning walk to work invigorated her, got her mind charged up for the day, but she was more than willing to let him drop her off at night.

They only spent about thirty minutes each day together, but with her schedule, it seemed to be the only time she spent with anyone outside the restaurant. At first, she'd been exhausted and silent. Getting a word out of her had been like pulling teeth. But slowly, she'd shared more of each day's drama. He got to hear about her employees, their lives, their problems. Customer issues. Supply holdups and new recipes. His responses often made her laugh, and she'd finally softened to him. He knew she was a believer and tried to get her to come to church with him, but she insisted that since Sunday was the only day the restaurant closed, she wanted to be alone, to rest, and read. She referred to it as "keeping the Sabbath," and it was her time of silence and solitude after six days of being "onstage."

Lindsey's rejection of his offer to take her to church had left a distinct but undefined pang in Jeff's chest—which was when he realized that he was falling for her. For someone who probably wouldn't return the emotion.

Maybe she *couldn't.* That thought stuck in his mind now as he watched her blue eyes focus on some far distance, beyond the recorder, beyond the walls. Her face barely moved, as if she'd been caught up in some long-ago event. He sat straighter, realizing why her behavior seemed familiar. He'd seen it, all too often, in other women....

Clarity of detail, but almost no emotion. Jeff frowned. At the hospital, Lindsey had been animated, as if still pumped on adrenaline. Now she hugged herself and revealed no emotion, almost as if she'd done this dozens of times. Combined with her lack of response to her own injuries, as if getting tossed around and beaten up happened to her frequently, Lindsey suddenly seemed less like an accident victim and more like a battered wife.

Or the battered child she'd been.

Jeff had heard about the abusive childhood

the three Presley girls—April, June and Lindsey—had endured and survived. Even though he didn't know all the details, what he did know made him seethe with rage toward their father. He had abused them all, eventually killing both his wife and son in drunken rages. *Is that what you're remembering now?* he silently asked her. *Is that what makes you keep a distance from everyone?*

An odd image flashed in Jeff's mind, and he blinked hard. An image of the GTO as it had pulled into the restaurant's parking lot and ground in a circle to face the exit again. *Distance.* He blinked again, tying to recall a mere glance at an image his police-trained mind had momentarily locked on.

The tag.

"Distance."

Ray and Lindsey faced him again. "What?" Ray asked.

Jeff tapped the desk, the image in full bloom in his mind now. "He said he'd driven down from Chicago, but Illinois requires a front license plate. The GTO had a University of Tennessee plate on the front…which would certainly explain the bright orange of the car."

Lindsey's eyes widened, and she grabbed

his forearm. "And his accent. More Tennessee than Chicago."

Ray made a note. "So we need to check records for GTOs in Tennessee only."

"And juvenile records, where we can. This kid's been in trouble before. No one that age starts by kidnapping a stranger."

Lindsey tightened her grip on his arm. "And the drugs. He was definitely hyped up on something. Drugs to make him brave and stupid enough to try something like this."

Ray glanced up at his deputy. "And you don't think he stole the car."

Jeff shook his head. "I think the older guy planned this and provided the car."

"And he's not happy about the wreck," Lindsey added.

Jeff stared at her. "Why do you say that?"

Lindsey shivered a bit and pulled back into herself again, crossing her arms over her stomach. "That GTO had been completely restored. You don't just *maintain* a car like that. It's been *babied*." She closed her eyes. "He said the kid deserved to die for wrecking it."

Jeff glanced once at Ray, then reached out and stroked her upper arm with the back of his hand. "You need to go home."

After a moment, she nodded. "And to the restaurant."

* * *

Lindsey breathed a sigh of relief to find that the Sheriff's Department had secured the restaurant. Ray had grabbed the deposit bag at the GTO and tossed it into evidence. He'd return it after they had fingerprinted it. Once again, Lindsey said a prayer of thanks that God had led her to answer her sister's wedding invitation, bringing her to the amazing small town of Bell's Springs, Tennessee.

Definitely a God thing. Exhaustion consumed every muscle, and with a sigh Lindsey leaned heavily against the back door of Ray's cruiser, looking out at the stars. She almost hadn't answered that invitation, thinking at first it had to be a joke. Their abusive father had kicked April and June out of the house after their mother and brother had died. When he went to prison, neither April nor June were anywhere to be found. Lindsey, just ten and still carrying her detested birth name of July, had felt betrayed and abandoned. She hadn't spoken to either of her sisters in the fifteen years that followed.

She couldn't believe that June would contact her after all that time. But a quick search on the internet brought up more information on both sisters than she'd thought possible, including a few details about the horrors they'd survived, and how they had thrived afterwards. April had survived an abusive spouse, and the people in her new hometown had helped her start a home-based business making jams and jellies. June, who had spent years on the street, had lost her first husband and been wrongly accused of murder. Now she ran a grant-writing business and authored a popular blog, *June's Bell County Wanderings,* which was an online diary of life in this small town. Curiosity had dissolved into an unexpected longing for family. Lindsey's anger at her sisters had vanished as she'd learned how difficult their own lives had been, how they'd fought to succeed. That they were both happily married now and living in a great community emboldened her with a hope she hadn't felt in a long time.

So Lindsey had come to Bell's Springs to reunite with her sisters, finding, in addition, a home for her own dreams.

"Penny for your thoughts." Beside her in the backseat, Jeff still watched her closely, his attention warming Lindsey's spirit.

"It's a God thing."

Jeff's eyebrows arched. "Say again?"

She smiled, suddenly aware of how odd her words must have sounded. "Sorry. Not—" she waved a hand between them, pointing to the bandages they both sported "—this. Tonight." She circled her hand in the air, then rested it on his arm. "All of it. Me being in Bell County. Finding a place for the restaurant so quickly."

Jeff looked down at her hand, his words soft as he repeated, "A God thing."

Puzzled, Lindsey watched him a few moments, then glanced in the rearview mirror at Ray. The sheriff studied his deputy, as well, his brows forming a single line over concerned eyes.

Why would this bother him? Lindsey turned again to Jeff, who clenched one fist, even as he placed the other hand tenderly over hers. Lindsey's breath caught a second at the gentleness of his touch in contrast to the troubled expression on his face. But no one spoke again until Ray turned into the drive of the cottage she called home. Jeff seemed to shake off whatever troubling thought had seized him as he looked up at Lindsey, a forced smile on his face. He squeezed her hand, then released it as he reached for the door.

"I'll walk you in, make sure you're safe."

"Sure," she answered. As soon as he got out, she whispered to Ray, "Is he going to be all right?"

"Physically, he'll bounce back quickly." Ray's expression remained stoic.

"Mentally?"

"He has a lot to work out."

"You ever been through anything like this?"

He nodded. "Every officer goes through it eventually. Part of the job. No one's per—" His words broke off as Jeff opened Lindsey's door.

Holding her crutch, he helped her out, then walked her to the narrow stoop at the front of her house. "What time will you leave for the restaurant?"

"Around four. Breakfast prep only takes an hour or so, and RuthAnn comes in at five to help."

"RuthAnn Crenshaw?"

She nodded.

"Anyone else?"

"Not till lunch."

"You stay all day, right?"

She shook her head. "Lunch is actually light for us. RuthAnn stays till after breakfast, around eight, then goes to her retail job in Springfield. She comes back in at five-thirty, stays till closing. Damon Schneider and his sister come in at eleven, but after lunch prep, I usually walk home and nap till three. The Schneiders stay till six, then RuthAnn and I work till we close at eight. I'm going to have to hire at least one more person soon, but for now, that's it."

He hesitated, a sudden wariness in his voice. "So where was RuthAnn tonight?"

Lindsey's eyes widened as she remembered. "She got a call just before seven. Someone said her mother had fallen. She took off like a shot."

Jeff's eyes hardened. "Did she say who called?"

"I'm not sure she knew. Do you think that had something to do—"

"I'll check it out."

Weariness flooded Lindsey's body, and she leaned heavily against the door frame. "Why is this happening?"

Jeff touched her shoulder. "Get some rest. Ray will run me home, then he'll be out here 'til you're ready to go. I'll relieve him and take you to the restaurant. You shouldn't walk."

"You really don't have to—"

"Lindsey." He interrupted her, then paused and let out a slow breath. "I know I didn't take care of you—"

Without thinking, she cupped his cheek with her free hand, stopping his words. "You did all anyone could do." The doubt in his eyes made Lindsey ache in a way she didn't quite understand, but she knew neither of them could deal with it now. Slowly, she eased her hand away. "I'll see you at four." Straightening and pulling open the screen door, Lindsey unlocked her home and reached in to turn on the light.

Then she screamed.

THREE

In the flash of a second following her scream, Lindsey both recognized the man standing in her living room and found herself staring at Jeff's back as he burst from behind her, blocking her from the intruder, gun drawn.

"Wait!" Her voice squeaked, barely audible, but Jeff had already realized that the abruptly terrified man in front of them posed no threat.

He lowered his gun. "Max, what are you doing in here?"

Ray shoved in behind them on full alert, only to have the same reaction. "Maxwell, we could have shot you."

Maxwell Carpenter, "Max" to everyone who'd known him for more than five minutes, stood with his arms in the air, wagging his hands furiously and rocking from one foot to the other. "I'm sorry, I'm sorry!" His glasses had slid down his nose, and he stared at them over the top of the black frames. "I was just worried about Lindsey.

I heard the ruckus on the scanner. The door was open, so I thought she was home, then realized it was all dark."

Lindsey shuddered as she noticed the two officers straighten.

"The door was open?" Jeff asked.

Max nodded, his hands still quivering in the air.

"Gage, clear the house," the sheriff ordered. "Max, put your arms down."

Jeff moved through the four small rooms of the house quickly, checking closets and under the bed.

His hands dropping to his side as if he'd held up barbells too long, Max focused on Lindsey. "You're hurt."

She smiled weakly. "Nothing serious. You really don't have to worry."

He shrugged one shoulder, causing a shock of dark hair to flop down over his forehead. He raked it back, his hands still shaking. "You're my favorite tenant, and I'm a dad. You're my Ashley's age. It's not exactly a habit that's easy to break."

Since moving into the small rental home, Lindsey's affection for Max grew almost daily. Max Carpenter bore not even a remote resemblance to her own father, but she began to see why some women could view their dads so fondly. She reached toward the older man as if to comfort him. "Max—"

"You should have called us." Ray Taylor apparently didn't totally accept Max's explanation. "You know better. You don't just walk in on your single female tenants alone, and if the door is open but no one's home, you call us. One could get you sued; the other could get you killed."

"Actually, both could get you killed," muttered Jeff as he returned to the living room, "given how many women in this county have carry permits." He glanced at Max, then at Ray. "All clear. Back door was still locked from the inside."

Ray nodded. "Lindsey, take a look around, see if anything is missing."

Max pushed his glasses up on his nose. "I didn't notice anything out of—"

"Lindsey." Ray's narrowed eyes stayed on Max, and his tone ended the conversation.

"Okay." Lindsey adjusted the crutch under her arm and limped past Ray, a little annoyed at her brother-in-law. Max had been good to her, and he'd never entered the house without giving her advance warning. In fact, Max had been her business mentor since she'd arrived here. Ray had no reason to be so…official. Still, she looked around the living room slowly, then shook her head. "Everything in here looks fine." She headed for her office, and Jeff followed.

The tiny home, with its living room, kitchen, two bedrooms and one bathroom, sat on a dead-end street along with eleven other identical houses, each one owned and rented by Max. The rents made up the bulk of his income, along with a small courier service he ran out of the converted house next door to Lindsey's restaurant. Lindsey used one of the bedrooms as an office, and now she paused, glancing over the paperwork on her desk. "Why is Ray suspicious of Max?"

Jeff hesitated and glanced over his shoulder. "I'm not sure."

"Max's been great to me. He even helped me with the business plan for the restaurant, especially with the stuff relating to Bell County and all the forms and regulations for the state." She turned and headed for the second door in the office. The house had no hallway, with each room directly adjacent to two others. The living room led to the office, which led to the bedroom. A walk-through bathroom separated the bedroom from the kitchen at the back of the house. An arch between the kitchen and living room made the area look bigger than it actually was.

Lindsey glanced around the bedroom and

shook her head. "Nothing's been touched." A flicker of light outside the window caught her eye, and she limped over. Her next-door neighbor was RuthAnn Crenshaw, who worked with her. Barely visible in the golden light of her windows, the older woman sat on her front stoop, her knees drawn up to her chest and one arm wrapped around her legs. A red spot glowed and faded as RuthAnn took a draw on a cigarette.

Lindsey scowled, and Jeff touched her elbow lightly. "What's wrong?"

"RuthAnn. She's never up this late. She's watching my house."

"You think she saw something?"

"Don't know. As far as I can tell, there was nothing to see. Nothing's been touched in here. I probably woke her up when I screamed. Or she was still awake because of her trip to her mother's. Her mom must be doing okay, or she wouldn't be back here."

As they watched, RuthAnn flicked the cigarette out in the yard, stood and went into her house. A second later, all the lights went off.

"I'll tell Ray—"

Lindsey turned. "Please don't bother her." She touched his arm. "I doubt RuthAnn saw anything. I probably just didn't latch the door firmly this morning. Sometimes I leave in such a hurry I don't check. When I do, the wind will pop it open."

"Lindsey—"

"Please. Her mom lives all the way over in Portland. She must be exhausted."

Jeff clinched his jaw, and Lindsey could see he struggled with her request. "I'll talk to her in the morning. I promise. If she saw anything, I'll call you."

He still scowled but finally relented, nodding just once. Satisfied, they finished the rest of her survey and returned to the living room, where Ray still held Max in his gaze, reminding Lindsey of a cobra captivating a bird.

The three men left, and Lindsey locked her front door and double-checked the back door dead bolt. She finished her nighttime routine, checking each of the windows one last time. A second cruiser sat next to Ray's, and Jeff got into it, letting her know Ray had changed his mind about leaving her alone for even a minute. Max, who lived with his family a couple of blocks away, was nowhere in sight.

Lindsey sighed. Although she didn't spend much time here, her cottage had become her refuge, her place of safety, where she recharged and prepared herself for another day. She'd filled it with inexpensive but comfortable furniture and decorated it with special touches of her own. A table runner that had belonged to her mother covered the top of the bookcase in the living room. After her mother's death, she'd gone into foster care. The comforter on her bed had been a gift from her foster mom when she'd headed off to culinary school.

Tonight, the cottage felt a little less safe, but despite the tension and trauma of the evening, Lindsey sank into bed, settling her ankle carefully and cherishing the soft embrace of her covers. Yet, even as tired as she was, she wouldn't relax without finishing her day the same way she had since she was a child. She plumped the pillows behind her, then turned to her bedside table, where she kept her Bible and music box side by side. Together with her mother's diary, which she kept tucked into a secret compartment of the music box, these made up the sole surviving mementos of her childhood. The Bible had belonged to her grandmother, and contained a treasure trove of family stories, sermon notes and memorabilia nestled in its pages.

Every night Lindsey read a passage from each one, then prayed about what she'd read and the events of the day. Now she muttered, "Lord, I hope you're ready for an earful tonight."

Never, baby girl, never hesitate to tell the good

Lord everything. He already knows it, just as He knows every hair on your head. But He'll want you to tell Him all the same. He wants to hear your heart.

Lindsey leaned back against the pillows, the voice of her mother echoing in her mind. As a child, she'd heard her mother pray, talking to God as if He were her best friend. Maybe He was... She didn't seem to have many others. *So what's in my heart tonight, other than people who want to kill me, hospitals and old GTOs?*

Jeff.

Lindsey opened her eyes and let out a deep sigh. She shook her head and pinched the bridge of her nose with two fingers. "No," she whispered. "I can't."

But she couldn't shake the way he'd looked at her at the police station, his expression determined and concerned, his touch gentle. The rich brown of his eyes had seemed to grow ever darker as she'd talked. One lock of his black hair always fell down over his forehead, and he pushed it back without thinking. Except for tonight. As he'd watched her, he hadn't seemed to notice his own injuries, and he'd never touched that strand of hair.

"But I'm just another case, right? Just one more citizen of the county he loves so much?"

Jeff did adore living in Bell County, and he often spoke of the people here as if he were personally charged with their welfare. And, maybe, in a way, he was. But even to her reluctant heart, the words sounded hollow.

"I just can't," she whispered to her walls. "I can't be more." She shook her head, trying to clear it of the image of the young deputy. "I need to stay focused. Dreams only come true with work." And right now, a relationship was not part of her dreams.

She sat a little straighter and reached for her Bible. Then she paused, her hand hovering over the black leather cover. Every night, Lindsey reached for the Bible in the same way, her hand clasping it just so. Tonight, however, the Bible was not the way she'd left it last night. She pulled back her hand, and a slight chill ran up her spine.

Nothing in the house had been touched. Except her grandmother's Bible.

Jeff waved one more time as the cruiser backed out of his driveway. After the warmth of the car, the post-midnight air gave him a slight chill. His head still throbbed, and every muscle felt as if it were on the edge of twitching, but there was a familiar comfort from just being at home. As he watched the taillights disappear over a low rise, a soft whimper made him turn and look down. He smiled. "Hey, buddy. Miss me?"

The golden Lab mix waited patiently on the bottom step of the staircase leading up to his over-the-garage apartment. At the sound of Jeff's voice, Charley's tail thumped wildly against the side of the garage.

"Yeah, me, too." Jeff rubbed Charley's head playfully, wincing from his injuries as he dropped down on the step next to his dog. He glanced toward his parents' house and, as he expected, their low ranch home lay still and silent. Darkness filled each window, although a dusk-to-dawn light bathed most of the yard in a harsh lavender-white light. Alan wouldn't get home for another couple of hours. Since her last bout with cancer, his mom always turned in early, and even though she'd been a nurse at one time, both Alan and Jeff were careful not to let their work intrude too much into her life these days.

Jeff hated to see how weak she'd become; his childhood memories were of a woman so vibrant and strong he thought she could take on the world. Alan had been a great stepdad, and when Alan was diagnosed with cancer, Jeff had come home from Los Angeles where he'd been working. He hadn't wanted to come back, but now he hoped he never had to leave. After he and Alan had converted the garage loft to a cozy studio, he'd settled in for good.

Jeff let out a long sigh and clutched Charley's ruff again. "I guess I've turned into a cliché, Charley-boy. The thirty-year-old man still living with his folks."

Charley obviously didn't mind. The huge fenced yard gave him plenty of running room, and the food and water were steady. Plus, he loved the occasional ride in the truck.

Jeff knew he should go upstairs, but as the painkillers from the hospital wore off, his head cleared. Despite the lingering headache, his memory had started to return with more details than he could recall earlier. He knew he should take more pills and rest, but at the moment, his thoughts bounced around in his head, going over the events of the night, seeing how many more details he could fill in.

Jeff remained amazed at how fast everything had happened—how his life, and Lindsey's, had changed almost in an instant. At just before eight o'clock, Jeff had checked on Lindsey, to see if she was ready to head for the bank. As usual, she was, and he waited for her outside. Less than thirty minutes later, Lindsey lay trapped in a wrecked GTO and he struggled to recover from being stunned twice in one night. Both stun-gun burns ached and itched, but he refused to rub them. Not many officers he knew had ever been stunned twice, much less during the same attack. One attack, two assailants. One scared and high, the other cruel and efficient.

Jeff stilled, resting his hand on Charley's back. Twice. The deep baritone of his second attacker's voice resonated in his head. A stranger's voice, one he'd never heard. Yet the man had addressed Jeff, talked about Lindsey, as if they were intimate friends. *How do you know us? How do you...*

...how did you know how to turn off the alarm?

Jeff stiffened. Lindsey had set off the alarm, yet it had been silent during the second attack. Turned off. Jeff looked down at Charley. "He knew the code. Wonder how many people have that code?"

Charley licked the excess drool off his lips and returned to panting, his eyes bright.

He made a mental note to ask Lindsey, grimacing again as he thought about her swollen jaw and twisted ankle. "She has no idea how lucky she was." Her account of the accident horrified him. She'd taken a desperate, risky chance, one that could easily have killed her. She took it, knowing that if the guy got to his destination, she'd be dead anyway.

The second attacker must have been on his way to that destination when he left Jeff. That's why he came on the wreck first, checking to see what happened. According to Lindsey's statement, he stole the paper from the boy, then groped for the glove compartment before the first responders chased him off.

The glove compartment…

Jeff looked down at Charley. "Wanna go for a ride?"

Charley heard the word "ride" and jumped from the steps with a soft woof. Jeff pushed up, ignoring his aches, and headed to the first door of the three-car garage. He punched a code into the keypad next to the door, and the middle door slid open with a low rumble. He opened the door of his pickup, and Charley hopped in as if it were the middle of the day. He settled into the passenger seat and let out another low bark.

"Yeah, I know it's late." Jeff reached for a jacket from behind the seat, knowing that Charley would want the window down. Plus, Troy's garage would be as cold, if not colder, than the air outside. He zipped it up, then got in and fastened his seat belt. "But I thought you might want to visit with Niki and Nora."

Charley wagged his tail, then pushed his nose against the window.

"Okay." Jeff started the truck's engine, then lowered the passenger window, grinning as it made Charley one happy, windblown dog.

The ride to the garage didn't take nearly as long as Charley would have liked. Although Alan and Elizabeth Gage lived on the far outskirts of town, everything in Bell's Springs was still pretty close together, unlike the two other, more spread out, small towns in the county. Fifteen minutes after he pulled out of the drive, he pulled up at the former gas station that was the front of Troy's garage. Troy had knocked out a wall and attached a Quonset hut to the back of the building, giving the place the oddest architecture in the county. It also meant the building was a mini–echo chamber, making sneaking up on Troy's two guard dogs impossible.

Jeff knew where Troy kept the building's spare key hidden, but a light from the office at the front of the building told him he might not need it. "Can't believe he's still at work," Jeff mumbled to Charley.

They got out of the truck, and Jeff rapped sharply on the front door. The resulting canine explosion from within told him that at least Niki and Nora were awake. So, apparently, was Troy, whose bass voice shortly joined those of the twin

Rottweilers. "This had better be good, if you know what's good for you!"

Jeff watched through the grease-coated front window as the big man emerged from the office and crossed the small waiting area. The wooden front door flew open, and Troy stared at Jeff through the screen door with a resigned expression. "Yeah, I had a feeling I'd be seeing you tonight." He glanced down at Charley. "You're going to turn these two into pets yet."

Jeff grinned. On either side of Troy, Niki and Nora wagged their tails and whined with pleasure.

"Well, come on in." Troy pushed open the screen and the three dogs rushed together in a tumble of playfulness, then dashed deeper into the building. An ominous crash sounded somewhere in the depths, but Troy shrugged it off. "I fix things for a living." He motioned with his head, and Jeff followed him into the office.

"I'm guessing Ray told you to stay away from here tonight, which is why it's so late." Troy settled into an ancient office chair, which groaned and creaked from the three hundred pounds on his six-foot-five frame. "Took you a while to argue yourself into it."

"What are you doing up anyway?" Jeff sat on a straight chair on the other side of Troy's desk.

He inhaled deeply, taking in the familiar smell of the garage—a combination of oil, grease, rubber and something indefinable that might have been sweat.

Troy winced. "Jen's sister and mother are in town. Thought I'd sleep here tonight."

"I thought you liked your mother-in-law."

"One on one, she's okay. But the three of them together are like something out of Shakespeare. 'Double, double, toil and trouble. Fire, burn, and cauldron'...whatever."

Jeff grinned. Troy liked to keep the facade of the redneck mechanic for his customers, but Jeff couldn't talk to him for long without being reminded that Troy had been an English teacher when he inherited the garage from his dad.

Troy went on. "Besides, with all the ruckus tonight, I figured either you or Ray would show up late to check out that GTO. Neither one of you can let something lie once you get your teeth into it." He shrugged again. "Gave me a chance to get caught up on some of my parts ordering."

"How's the GTO look?"

Troy hesitated, watching Jeff closely. "You know they had to use the Jaws of Life to get her out, right?"

Jeff paused. He hadn't. In fact, he hadn't wanted

to think too much about the wreck itself. Just seeing Lindsey's injuries had been hard enough.

Troy apparently saw the conflict in Jeff's face. He nodded. "Got it. Just wanted you to know that not all the damage to the car was from the accident. I know you've seen a lot of wrecked cars, but it's always different when it's someone you care about."

Jeff took a deep breath. "Where is it?"

Troy stood. "In the back bay. That's the most secure. Farthest from the door and the closest to the dogs' bed."

Troy led the way back through the waiting area and through what had been the original garage for the gas station. The smells of grease and oil grew stronger as they passed under two SUVs up on lifts and through double swinging doors into the Quonset hut. This was where most of the bodywork took place, and five of the six bays held vehicles in for insurance repairs. On the far side of a van that looked as if it had gotten up close and personal with a tree sat the orange GTO, its roof half peeled back and the passenger door missing. The shattered and crushed front end had compressed the big engine back toward the firewall, and blood spatters were all over the spiderwebbed windshield and twisted steering wheel.

Jeff's stomach lurched. He had seen hundreds of accident scenes, but Troy had been right. It was different when someone you care about had been inside that much destruction. To think of Lindsey shoved into that tiny space beneath the dash...

"From what the guys said at the site, the blood's mostly the boy's, not Lindsey's."

Jeff didn't respond at first, then turned to look over his shoulder as another flurry of barking came from the front of the shop.

"Now what?" Troy turned and headed back to the front of the shop, leaving Jeff to stare at the ruined GTO. He knew he shouldn't touch it without gloves, but the urge to reach out to the ripped metal was irresistible. He hesitated, feeling one more time the ache of failure. If he'd done his job, she wouldn't have gone through this.

"Man," he mumbled to himself, "you've messed up with women before, but this time you fouled up with her and everyone else. She won't look at you twice now. She shouldn't."

"Is this what you call doing things by the book, Deputy Gage?"

Jeff swung around, coming face-to-face with Sheriff Ray Taylor. At his side, leaning hard on her crutch, stood Lindsey.

FOUR

Lindsey couldn't speak. Her mind felt as empty of thought as Jeff's face was of color. They stood, Ray's harsh words hanging in the air between them.

Finally, Jeff straightened, drawing himself almost to attention. "No, sir."

After another beat of silence, Ray spoke, his voice a bit less commanding. "You know where I keep the gloves in my cruiser?"

Jeff didn't move. "Yes, sir."

"Go get them."

"Yes, sir."

Jeff didn't salute, but he might as well have, thought Lindsey, watching him go. His gaze never met hers.

Troy sniffed. "Boy's wounds run deep, Ray."

Ray nodded once. "More than I realized. He shouldn't be here. He should be in bed with a screaming headache, not obsessing about this."

Lindsey looked from one man to the other, her mind beginning to clear. "What does that mean?"

Troy ran his hand through his graying hair. "It means, dear lady, that cops aren't like the rest of us. Things hit them differently than they do us. And it would probably be best if we all act like we didn't hear his last words before he saw us. He needs to work off that sense of failure."

Ray made a low rumbling noise in the back of his throat but remained silent.

Lindsey felt more confused than ever, but didn't have a chance to ask anything more. Jeff strode back into the garage with a box of latex gloves in one hand, which he held out toward Ray. Ray plucked out two pair and handed one to Lindsey. As she pulled one glove over her hand, the golden Lab she'd met earlier at the front of Troy's garage walked up to Jeff. The dog looked up at him and whimpered softly.

Jeff didn't look down at first. He pulled out a pair of gloves, then set the box on the fender of the van in the next bay. The Lab whined, still staring up at him. Jeff hesitated, then looked down at the dog, his expression softening a bit. "I'm okay, boy, I promise."

The Lab responded by pressing against his thigh.

Lindsey's chest tightened inexplicably, and she found her voice. "Is he yours?"

Jeff nodded but didn't look up.

"What's his name?"

"Charley."

The Lab beat his tail twice at the sound of his name.

"He's beautiful."

Jeff finally looked at her, his face calm, his eyes narrowed a bit with curiosity. "Thanks."

"He brought Charley over to play with Niki and Nora," Troy said.

"That's pretty cool."

Ray cleared his throat, which broke the mood, and Troy snapped his fingers, calling to Charley. "C'mon, boy, you and I need to get back out front with the girls."

"Go on," Jeff whispered, and Charley turned and followed Troy out of the hut.

"You ready?" Ray asked.

Jeff nodded curtly, then snapped on the gloves and pulled a small notebook from his pocket. Lindsey approached the GTO with them, standing as close to them as she dared. They examined the outside first, and as they walked around the car, Ray pointed to one of the taillights.

"Have you asked Troy about replacement parts?"

Jeff shook his head and made a note. "We hadn't got that far yet."

They continued the examination inside. Ray

pulled a small flashlight from his belt and pointed it at different parts, with Jeff making notes about each bit of damage. Lindsey moved to one side, trying to peer around them, although she had no idea what they were looking for.

"Lindsey," Ray asked, "did he say anything else?"

She took a deep breath, trying to remember. "Not him, no. Just kept mumbling about turning left. The other guy did most of the talking." She adjusted the crutch under her arm, shuddering a bit at the memory.

Jeff caught her motion and stepped away from the car. He unzipped his coat, slipped it off, and draped it around her shoulders. He moved so smoothly and quickly that Lindsey barely had time to react—or refuse.

"Thank you," she whispered, watching his face closely.

But he'd put up his guard. "It's cold in here."

Lindsey nodded. "We left the house so fast, I forgot to grab a jacket."

"Why did you come here?"

Lindsey shrugged one shoulder. "Couldn't sleep. Couldn't stop thinking about this car."

"Everything was peaceful," Ray mumbled. "Next thing I know, she's knocking on my car, insisting that we come over here." They went back to work, Jeff looking over Ray's shoulder and taking notes.

Ray saved the glove compartment for last, but it wouldn't budge. Jeff pulled a screwdriver from a nearby shelf, and the lid popped down with little resistance. From inside they removed a plastic-wrapped cluster of papers and a wrinkled, crumbling copy of *Catcher in the Rye.* They all arched their eyebrows at that discovery.

Ray turned it over a couple of times. "That's probably been in there since 1968."

Jeff looked down at the paperwork. "I can see at least one registration form in here."

Ray nodded. "Probably what he was trying to get." Jeff started to open the plastic, but Ray stopped him. "Not here. I want it opened under better conditions."

Lindsey's frustration bit at her. "Y'all are driving me crazy."

They looked at each other, then at her. "We have to do this—"

She waved a hand to cut Ray off. "I know, I know. Doesn't mean I like it, though. I just want to know who's doing this."

Jeff handed the packet to Ray. "So do we. That's why I came. To see what he was after in the glove box. But those papers may not have any answers. Or they just may be the beginning. Either way, we can't act on the information tonight. But at least we now know what he was after, and we can keep it safe. I just couldn't sleep knowing something important had only Niki and Nora to guard it."

"Even though you came unprepared to collect it," Ray said.

Jeff let out a long breath. "Part of my addled thinking, I guess. Troy probably has some—"

Ray stopped his words by sharply clearing his throat. "We'll talk later."

Ray pointed from Jeff to Lindsey. "I need you to take her home. I have a couple of evidence bags in the cruiser. I'll get these locked up at the station, then be back at her house to relieve you. You both need as much sleep as you can get before that monstrous hour she plans to start breakfast." Without giving either of them a chance to respond, Ray strode out of the garage, disappearing through the double doors.

Lindsey and Jeff looked at each other. Jeff, who still had a slightly wary look in his eyes, glanced away first, focusing on the screwdriver in his hand. He juggled it lightly, then replaced it on the shelf, turning away from her.

Lindsey took a deep breath and broke the ice with, "Well, I guess that's—oops!" She jumped, startled by the cold nose suddenly thrust into the hand at her side. She struggled for balance, stumbling a bit with the crutch and grabbing Charley's ruff at the same time.

"Charley!" Jeff was at her side immediately, one hand on her elbow.

Lindsey let him help her find her balance, then pulled Charley close to her thigh. "He didn't mean it."

"I know, but he can be demanding when it comes to getting petted." He gazed affectionately at Charley. "He doesn't like the word 'No.'"

"I can relate."

"You do share a certain determination with him."

Lindsey grinned. "June tells me I give a whole new definition to the word *stubborn*."

"I can believe it." Jeff let out a long sigh, then offered her his arm. "Will you let me help you maneuver through the maze of Troy's shop?"

"I'd be honored."

"Let's put this on first." He helped her slip her arms into his jacket, then she grasped his arm as they left the Quonset hut and exited out the front. He waved at Troy, who was still staring at the computer in his office. "Lock up after us!" Jeff called.

"Will do. Get some sleep!"

Outside, Jeff escorted Lindsey to the passen-

ger door of a large black pickup. He held the
door open, and pointed to a handle on the frame.
"Grab that. It'll give you more stability." She did,
and Jeff helped boost her into the truck as easily
as if she'd been a young child.

His strength startled her. Lindsey had never
realized how fit Jeff was. Unlike his boss, who
wore fitted uniforms, Jeff wore his shirt loose,
almost a size too big. She'd never caught sight
of his broad, no doubt muscular chest, nor had
she ever felt it. In the six months of their friendship, they had never even hugged. Though they'd
laughed and chatted, they'd kept their distance.
For some reason that had seemed important.

"You in good?"

She settled herself in the seat and nodded. Jeff
closed the door and walked around the front of
the truck. She fastened the seat belt and closed
her eyes. The cab had a scent similar to Jeff's
cruiser—a light cologne, gun oil and leather—
mixed with something else, which Lindsey didn't
identify until Charley hopped up in the cab next
to her. Ah, she thought. Dog.

She wrapped one arm around the Lab and
tugged him close as Jeff started the engine.
"Does Charley ride with you a lot?"

He backed the truck away from the building.
"Almost every time I go out in the truck. He

thinks if it leaves, so does he. I think everyone in town knows Charley."

She hugged the dog, taking comfort in his solid warmth. "Sounds like a good friend to know."

Jeff didn't respond for a second. "Did you ever have dogs?"

Lindsey shook her head. "Not as a kid, but I always loved them and I played with all the neighborhood dogs. When I lived in Chicago I had a Poodle—Crimson—until I realized that a dog and a restaurant career weren't a good mix. Twelve hours in a kitchen didn't leave me with much time or energy for walks or play. I wound up giving her to a lawyer who worked out of her home."

"Did you miss her?"

"Like a best friend. I tried a cat, but it wasn't the same. We did *not* get along."

Jeff grinned. "So you're a dog person?"

Lindsey returned the smile. "I guess so. Or maybe I just ended up with a cranky cat."

"Maybe. We have a working cat."

Lindsey's curiosity arched. "A working cat?"

"My stepdad has a workshop in our garage, and we live in what is basically a big field. Mel keeps down the critter population, and she lives mostly outdoors or in the shop. She comes inside only during the winter, but she begs to get out a lot."

"Mel? You have a female cat named Mel?"

He chuckled as he turned the corner and started down the street toward her cottage. "It gets worse. Alan named her Melchior, after one of the Nativity Magi, because she's always bringing us gifts of grouse, mouse and mole."

Lindsey laughed. "That's awesome."

"Yeah, well, my mother didn't think so the first time she walked out on the deck barefoot."

Lindsey cringed. "Ew."

"Welcome to country living."

"I should hire Mel to take care of the restaurant."

"You have mice?"

"Not yet. But it's one of the things we have to stay constantly on guard for. Our nonperishable stores are a magnet for all sorts of unwanted critters."

They fell silent as Jeff turned the truck into the short driveway of her home. They looked at the house for a few moments, with every light blazing.

Jeff's voice softened. "Why did y'all really come to the garage?"

Lindsey stroked Charley's head absently, watching her home. "I couldn't sleep. I kept replaying everything in my head, over and over. I started to obsess about what he wanted out of the glove compartment until I came out and begged Ray to take me over there."

"I'm surprised he agreed."

Lindsey smirked, remembering the argument. "He didn't. I told him I'd walk, and he threatened to arrest me for obstruction. I told him if he did, he'd be the one to explain it to June."

Jeff nodded. "Yep. I can see why he gave in."

"I promised not to touch anything. To let him go over the car. How did you wind up there? I thought you were hurt so bad you'd be out for the night."

Jeff flexed his fingers around the wheel, then tightened his grip again. "I have a screaming headache and it hurts to breathe. The burns ache. But I've worked with worse, and as my head cleared of the painkillers, I didn't want to take them again." He paused. "I would have thought the same thing about you—that you were too hurt. I guess, when you've been through something like this..." His voice trailed off.

Lindsey's words were almost as soft. "You want resolution. You want answers."

"Have you...have you been the victim of a crime before?"

The images of everything she'd survived had

been swirling in her head all night, an unstoppable kaleidoscope. "Yes. Several times."

He flexed his hands again. "I haven't. When I'm investigating, unanswered questions spur me to the next step. As a victim—"

"—they're maddening." She reached across Charley and grasped Jeff's forearm. "It's also a lack of control. I've seen this in Ray. As a law enforcement officer there's an illusion of control because you're following the evidence. But the victim is usually in the dark. No idea what comes next. If you can let go of the idea that you can do anything to control what comes next, there's a peace you can find that opens up all possibilities."

He nodded a moment, then shook his head. "I'm not sure I can do that. I'm pretty desperate to find answers."

"So I wasn't the only one who wanted to snatch that packet out of Ray's hands and tear into it?"

Jeff laughed. "Nope." He released his seat belt. "Let's get you inside. You might be able to get— what—two hours of sleep?"

"Almost three."

He smiled. "Party girl." He opened the door and slid out, telling Charley to stay put. Then he opened her door and they reversed the process, with him bracing her as she eased down out of the truck and balanced herself against her crutch. She held his arm as they hobbled toward her front door, which she unlocked and pushed open. She waited as he did a quick check of the house, then stopped him as he returned with an "all clear." "Say, 'I refuse.'"

He scrunched his brow in puzzlement. "What?"

"Remember: 'I refuse to give up, give in, give over. I refuse to be defeated. He won't win.' Anytime you think you've fouled up everything, just say, 'I refuse.' God's listening, and you never know who else is."

Jeff straightened, recognition brightening his eyes. "I will." He reached out and touched her cheek lightly. "Good night, party girl."

She smiled, and went inside, closing the door behind her. She bolted the lock, then listened as Jeff's footsteps retreated off the porch. As she stood there, Lindsey realized the faint aroma of his cologne lingered on her shirt. She sighed. She might not be ready for a relationship, but Jeff Gage certainly had found a special place in her life.

Still, she'd been a victim before, and she had a strong feeling that their lives were about to be turned upside down.

* * *

Jeff sat in his truck, watching Lindsey's cottage until all the lights went out. Her words lingered in his mind, bringing both embarrassment and encouragement. Obviously, she'd overheard his words about how badly he had failed tonight…and thought he could work past it. He glanced at Charley. "What do you think, buddy?"

Charley barked, although Jeff couldn't tell if that meant he liked Lindsey or would like to have the window down. He started the engine and lowered the window, just as Ray pulled up beside him.

The sheriff got out and came over to the truck. "How's she doing?"

"As well as could be expected. Did you go back for that knife in the glove box?"

Ray nodded. "Troy was still up. I got it boxed and ready for processing. But I don't think you should do this one. I want to send it to the TBI lab."

Jeff stared at his boss, that nagging sense of failure looming. Had he messed up that bad? "Why?"

Ray took a deep breath. "I opened it. There was what looked like dried blood at the bottom of the blade, down in the slit. That knife has seen a lot of violence."

"You think we did right, not letting her see it?"

Ray hesitated. "I'm sure she'll sleep easier thinking he was reaching for paperwork instead of a ten-inch switchblade. Wish I could."

"With a blade like that, anyone could get close enough to kill her."

"Then we'd better pray he won't try anything in public."

"Pray. And stay close."

"Amen, brother. Now you try to sleep, as well."

Jeff headed back to his apartment, along streets with silent homes, gentle breezes. The illusion of safe, country living. He put his truck in the garage, and he and Charley retreated to his apartment. He sank into bed and drifted off, with his gun nearby.

FIVE

Feeling strangely refreshed following last night's events at the garage, even with little sleep, Lindsey went through her morning routine and dressed for the day. She never wore makeup for work, but she brushed her hair thoroughly before gathering it into a ponytail.

She stared in the mirror at the bruises and cuts on her face. Her whole body still ached from the night's ordeal, and her ankle still throbbed. But she couldn't cook breakfast on painkillers. She'd just have to cope with it. She told herself that if Jeff could do it, so could she. As she sat on the bed to put on her shoes, she touched her Bible one more time. Last night, she'd managed to convince herself that she'd moved it, probably when she'd made her bed. She hadn't mentioned it to Jeff, feeling a bit silly. Now she looked at it again. *I did move it. I must have.* With a sigh, she stood.

She was limping toward the door when a stark rapping on it forced a startled yelp out of her.

"You all right in there?"

Expecting it to be Ray or Jeff, Lindsey grinned at the much higher-pitched voice. June. She tugged open the door to find her older sister standing on the other side of the screen door, a thermos in one hand. "You just startled me."

June returned the grin and wagged the thermos. "Coffee. Brought some over for Ray a couple of hours ago. Thought you might want some on the way to work. As well as an extra hand when you got there." June pointed at the crutch. "Since you're a hand and foot short today."

Lindsey laughed. "Good morning to you, too."

June rocked up on her toes, then back. "You're lucky I let you sleep. Ray had to threaten me to keep me from busting in here and leaping on you for details and to tell me you were okay. Come on. Now you can tell me at work. Let me help you down the steps. Ray ordered Jeff to the station when he wakes up, but he already has one of the guys waiting for you at the diner. Ray's about ready to hit the sack. I keep telling him he's too old for these all-nighters, but he never listens."

Lindsey listened to her sister's prattle, loving every word. She wrapped an arm around

June's shoulders and together they eased down the steps. "Ray's not that old."

"Of course not. I'd just prefer he be home in bed with me than sitting in a cold car all night."

The man in question got out and opened the rear door of the cruiser. With June and Lindsey both settled in the backseat, they headed for the diner, June chattering the entire way about the latest happenings in town. Lindsey, grateful for the distraction, took in each word as they passed through the silent, empty streets of Bell's Springs. The trip to the Coffee-Time Café didn't take long, and they waved at the waiting sheriff's deputy as they moved slowly from Ray's car into the restaurant.

The converted four-square house had been a failed burger joint before Lindsey purchased it, knowing from her demographic research that a coffee shop with short orders and a full breakfast menu would do better than a burger place. She'd made adjustments to the place before opening six months ago, and she'd reorganized the kitchen to make it truly her own. So far, her changes had proved successful.

Lindsey paused just inside the kitchen, as she always did, closed her eyes, and took a deep breath. "Thank You, Lord, for all this." She exhaled slowly, then inhaled again, relishing the layers of scents that made up her restaurant. *Her* restaurant. Coffee, fried meat, fresh bread, sweet pastries.

Ray and June waited as she finished her prayer. Then Ray kissed his wife goodbye, and June came to Lindsey's side. "You perch and tell me what to do."

Lindsey slid onto a stool and propped her foot on the lower shelf of a worktable. "Are you sure about this? I know your grant-writing business has been picking up."

June waved away the concern. "I'll make it up tonight. Let's get to work."

Lindsey took a deep breath. "Let's start by emptying the fridge. I'll chop, mix and scramble while you start the coffee. RuthAnn will be in around five, and she can get us open and take the orders. You ever wait tables?"

"Many times. I'm not a bad short-order cook, either."

Lindsey nodded, then paused. "Thank you."

June trotted over and gave Lindsey a quick hug. "I'm just glad I'm here for you. April said she'd help, too, if you need her. She's not feeling well this morning, but she'll be over shortly."

"Good. She can bring me a case of strawberry preserves. I'm almost out. My customers love that I'm buying local—and that it's my sister's organic jams and jellies on the table."

They continued to chat back and forth as they worked, and Lindsey realized that June's presence, as frenetic as it could be at times, calmed her. Despite their years apart, despite their past animosity, they were still sisters.

At ten minutes after five, Lindsey glanced at the clock, then the back door, for the tenth time. *Where's RuthAnn? She's never this late.*

"Want me to call RuthAnn this time?"

Lindsey shook her head. "I'll do it. She was up late last night, too. She probably just overslept and can't hear the phone. I hope she hasn't had to go back to her mom's."

But, again, RuthAnn's phone rang until it switched to voice mail. Lindsey's stomach tightened as she hung up. "I don't like this."

June, deeply involved with the second batch of biscuit dough, nodded toward the parking lot. "Want me to ask the deputy to check on her?"

Lindsey shook her head and followed her instinct. Flipping open her cell again, she dialed Jeff.

He answered in the middle of the first ring. "What's wrong?"

"Nothing, I hope. RuthAnn isn't here yet. Could you—"

"On my way."

Every bit of the previous night's tension returned, settling over Lindsey as she tapped a pen on the worktable, the grocery list she'd been working on forgotten.

Behind her, June washed her hands, then slid a pan of biscuits into the oven. She walked over and put her arm around Lindsey's shoulders. "Want me to call April?" she asked softly.

After a moment, again following a dark, street-savvy instinct, Lindsey nodded. As June made the call, Lindsey slid off the stool and headed for her office. Time to get the cash drawer out of the safe and ready for the day. She had to open by 5:30 a.m., when the first farm workers and early-bird commuters would arrive.

"She'll be here in twenty minutes or so." June took the cash drawer from Lindsey and followed her to the counter in the customer section of the diner, helping Lindsey get the register up and running. Then, precisely on time, June unlocked the front door and greeted the first guests. She took orders, poured coffee and worked the register and drive-through, while Lindsey hobbled about in the back, cooking and filling plates.

April arrived just before six and took over the kitchen, insisting that Lindsey stay behind the register. Even though they'd never worked together before, the sisters quickly fell into a routine, calling back and forth, engaging in an ongoing banter that amused the customers.

Jeff arrived, alone, at 7:10 a.m., two hours after

Lindsey had called him. He waited for her in the kitchen, and from the dark circles around his eyes, she could see that he'd slept little—and still had not taken his pain medicine. He delivered the news without preamble.

"RuthAnn's gone."

The pit of Lindsey's stomach dropped. "Gone? How?"

He shook his head. "Her car's gone, but not her clothes or her suitcases. The place looks rough. Ransacked."

"You mean, like she was kidnapped?"

He took a deep breath and rested one hand on his gun. "We don't think she left of her own free will. RuthAnn was taken out by force."

The yellow crime scene tape stretched across RuthAnn's yard twisted and fluttered in the night wind, shuddering like a terrified rabbit. The full moon and bright streetlights cast a harsh glare across the lawn and abandoned house. Stark shadows from the few young trees in the area streaked the walls and grass.

Lindsey stared at the house, hugging herself against the chill. "I can't believe someone took her."

Jeff walked up behind her, standing so close she could feel the warmth of his body. "It may not be related. RuthAnn moved here a few years ago, but she grew up over in Portland. We're still looking into her past."

Lindsey closed her eyes and braced herself on her crutch, fighting the urge to lean back against Jeff. "I hate that she might be hurt because of me, and I don't want it to be because of her past, either. I just want her to be all right."

He paused. "We have to keep all options open until the evidence reveals something. How did it go today?"

Lindsey sighed and opened her eyes again. RuthAnn's house hadn't changed. Lindsey felt the chill more than ever and shivered. She just wanted everything to go back to normal. "Pretty well. June and April functioned like a team. The Schneiders came in on time, but June and April stayed all day. Did you find out about RuthAnn's mom?"

Jeff slipped off his jacket and draped it around her shoulders. "Her mom did fall, but she didn't break anything. They took her to the E.R., but they sent her home. RuthAnn stayed for a while, then came back here."

She closed one hand on the collar, her fingers brushing his as she twisted to look at him with a sad smile. "Thanks. This is getting to be a habit. Maybe I should take a coat."

"I don't mind."

She believed him. Lindsey tugged the jacket a little closer around her and glanced back at the house. "You know people often think Ruth-Ann's my mom."

His brow furrowed. "Why?"

"Well, we do have the same build, the same hair color, similar facial structure. The age difference is right, so it makes sense, if you think about it. We work together, and most people never look as closely as they should."

Jeff watched her for a few moments, his brows furrowed. Lindsey almost smiled. She loved that look on his face. Beneath his brows, his eyes had an intense focus and his lips tightened. He reminded her of a little boy studying a new puzzle. "What is it?"

"Lindsey, this may not be about you at all. Normally, we leave the diner first while she locks up. But not last night."

Her eyes widened. "You think he was after RuthAnn?"

He nodded and pulled his cell phone out of his pocket. "He didn't expect me to be there. Or you. If RuthAnn had been there, we'd have left a few minutes earlier. The stun gun was meant for RuthAnn. Ray?" He turned his attention to the phone and filled the sheriff in on their conversation. "I think we should look at the evidence, maybe even RuthAnn's house, with a new perspective. Right. Okay. Tomorrow." He hung up.

Lindsey grinned. "You wake him up?"

Jeff's cheeks pinked. "Something like that."

"He came by the restaurant about seven or so. He and June had supper in my office, then I made them leave. They're basically still newlyweds, but they don't get a lot of time together."

"Not lately, no. Usually around here crime is mostly drugs, car accidents and family squabbles—sometimes all three in the same location. But it's been active lately. Kinda hoping some of this cooler weather will chill people out."

"Have you had supper?"

Jeff's eyes widened. "Not really. I can grab something at home."

"Are you sure? I know it's late, but I could whip up something before your relief gets here. And, y'know, if this is about RuthAnn, y'all won't have to keep watch over me."

"Oh, we'll keep that on for a while. Until we're sure."

"Okay. Anyway, I do make a mean grilled cheese…" Lindsey's voice trailed off. She didn't know what to say next, or even why she'd impulsively asked him about dinner anyway. *Why did I do that?*

"I shouldn't. I mean, I like grilled cheese and all, and I'm sure you make a great one, but I need to stay outside."

"Sure. You probably should."

The sound of tires on gravel saved both of them as Jeff's replacement for the night drove into Lindsey's driveway. They left RuthAnn's and headed back to Lindsey's. After he made sure her house was secure, they walked outside, pausing just before they split up, with her heading back into the house and him to his car.

"Oh, here." She slipped the jacket off her shoulders and handed it back to him. "Thanks again."

"No problem. See you at four?"

She nodded, then headed into the house, feeling more than a little foolish. She shut the door, locking it as his cruiser backed out of the drive. She leaned against the door, banging her head lightly against it. "You're such a doofus," she told herself. "That was awkward. And dumb."

And confusing, especially since she knew he wanted more from her than she was ready to give. Yes, Jeff Gage had opened a door for her, had made a place for himself in her life. But she still wanted to wait. The restaurant—her dream—had to come first. Didn't it?

With a long sigh, Lindsey straightened and

adjusted the crutch under her arm. She didn't really need it; walking without it was uncomfortable but not impossible. She'd certainly had bad sprains before, and this didn't even come close. One, which happened when her father pushed her off their front porch, had put her on crutches for four weeks.

Still…being on her feet all day had left her ankle swollen and achy. She hobbled into the bathroom, slowly and carefully took a cool shower to wash away the day's restaurant grime, then slipped into her softest pajamas.

Bracing her back against the headboard and her foot on a pillow, Lindsey lifted the lid on the music box. The tinkling minuet relaxed her, and she opened her grandmother's Bible, turning to one of her favorite passages in 1 Samuel. The story of Abigail and David. Her mother loved it, as well, describing it as the moment when "an intelligent woman with a heart *for* God met a wise man who sought the heart *of* God."

"Would be nice to meet a man like that," Lindsey muttered, "but I hear they're few and far between." A thought flared in her mind that Jeff was such a man, but she tamped it down. Not yet. Setting the Bible aside, she leaned back, closed her eyes and prayed. Her words came slowly at first, as she thanked God for the blessings of that day.

Her mother had taught her that. That every day, no matter how horrid, also came with blessings, good things. When you could count the blessings, everything else would fall into perspective. *God's perspective,* she always said, *is not ours. We must focus on the fact that He sees the bigger picture.*

Lindsey always started with the simple ones—the smiles of her customers, the fact that they came often enough that she could afford this cottage—and moved on to ones that made every day better—the love of her sisters. The blessings came faster as she thanked God for each one and praised Him. Finally, she asked for His help, ending with a soft, "A few clues would be nice."

Lindsey opened her eyes again, reaching for the music box and the diary carefully hidden in the compartment underneath. Her mother had concealed it there, so her abusive husband couldn't find it. Lindsey had never felt the need to change that, even though she read from the diary every night. For no reason she could explain, Lindsey didn't want her mother's private thoughts exposed for the world's viewing.

She flipped through the book, tonight turning to the end, a section she'd read only once in all these years. Once had been hard enough; she'd never wanted to see those words again. But now she felt drawn to that passage, and she realized she needed to face it again. Without really knowing why, Lindsey took a deep breath and began reading.

August 7
July's hurt. He's been at my baby again. Bad this time... I think more in her mind than her body. She's always told me about the hurts before, but not now. I think she saw something he didn't want her to see.

Don't know when it happened. I came home from Mama's this afternoon and found her crying in the garage, hiding under a box. She wouldn't come out, screaming that she hated me, hated him, hated everything. But I couldn't leave her there. Her lip was messed up, and her eye. He'd torn a chunk out of her hair, and she was wet, head to toe, like she'd been dunked in a pool with all her clothes on. I dragged her out, scratching and fighting, then just held her tight until she calmed down. Still wouldn't tell me what happened, just turned sullen. I fixed her up best I could. She holed up in the girls' room for a bit.

Then I found him in our room. Scared me half to death. Didn't know he was there. But he was passed out, drunker than all get out. He looked awful, too, like someone had done to him what he's done to us. Messed up his eye real bad, cut face, arms all black-and-blue, cuts on his chest.

I know it'll be bad when he wakes up. I packed the girls up and took them to Mama's. She'll keep them for a few days. Wait for this one to blow over. He's still out. Been almost twelve hours.

Lindsey closed the diary and bit her lower lip, trying not to cry, remembering the days that followed that last entry. Two days later, the cops showed up at her grandmother's house to explain that the girls' mother had been carried to the hospital by a neighbor. His rage consuming him, their father had slammed her head into the refrigerator. She lived, but was never quite the same after that. She never wrote in the diary again. One horrific year later, she died at the hands of the man she found too terrifying to leave, and Lindsey ended up in foster care.

"Why, Mama? Why did you stay? Why?" Lindsey lost her fight against the tears, and the diary slipped from her lap as she surrendered to her tears.

* * *

Lindsey screeched, jerking awake. Gasping for air, she clutched the sheets, panting in the wake of the nightmare. The GTO had been powering toward RuthAnn. Lindsey's sweat-drenched pajamas stuck to her skin, and she pushed the sheets back and swung her legs out of bed, still taking in great gulps of air. "Dear Lord," she whispered. "What was *that?*"

A nightmare, definitely, but the images flooded her again as she sat, clutching the edge of the mattress. Her father's battered, slashed face. The GTO, peeling out with a deafening howl, aiming for RuthAnn, who merely stood there, twirling her keys.

Lindsey looked up. "Her keys." RuthAnn had a duplicate set of keys to the restaurant. She also had a set for Lindsey's house, just as Lindsey had a set for RuthAnn's. "In case of emergency," she'd said. "Neighbors look out for each other."

She glanced at the clock: 2:30 a.m. No use in going back to sleep now. Lindsey stood up, limping around her bedroom as she peeled off the pajamas. After a quick shower to wash off the sweat, Lindsey dressed for work, a thought nagging at her.

The keys. RuthAnn's house had been ransacked, but whoever did this probably wouldn't have found them, thanks to RuthAnn's foolproof hiding place. But now the house stood unsecured, with the front door closed but the lock smashed. Lindsey suddenly felt a vulnerability she had not experienced in a long time, and she rolled her shoulders, trying to shake off the twinge that hovered there. Her back tensed, and she fought the urge to look behind her. Whoever got those keys could get to her or her restaurant at any time. *I need to retrieve those keys.*

She propped the crutch against the back door, leaving it behind, then took the three back steps one foot at a time. At the bottom, she tested her balance and stability on the wet grass. Perfect.

Moving carefully and favoring her ankle, Lindsey limped the short distance between the two houses with no problem. Using her own key, she opened the back door, slipped under the crime scene tape and stepped into the kitchen. The kitchen light still burned, casting harsh shadows over the wreckage in the kitchen. Dishes had been flung from the cabinets, as well as food, utensils and cookware. The smell of rancid vegetables and rotten meat permeated the air, and Lindsey grimaced. "Oh, Ruthie."

She shut the door, wincing again, as she looked down. Shattered glass blended with streaks of flour and sugar, and both ground beneath Lindsey's shoes as she stepped forward. "Ruthie, I'm sorry, but I have to do this."

She took a deep breath to steady her nerves. "Now," she whispered, "let's see if those hiding places are as good as you thought."

Lindsey stepped as carefully as possible through the debris on the floor as she headed for the kitchen sink. Pulling open the doors underneath, Lindsey ran her hand up against the panel at the front, which was above the doors but below the sink.

"Yep," she muttered, as her hands closed around the small key ring of her house keys dangling from a strip of duct tape. "I thought you were crazy, but you were right." She remembered well the day RuthAnn told her about the hiding place.

Shoving her house keys deep into her pocket, she headed for the bedroom in search of the restaurant keys. RuthAnn's house was identical to Lindsey's, and the light from the kitchen provided enough light for her to see that the destruction was just as bad there. Pillows lay ripped open, the mattress pushed off her bed. Ceramic shards littered the floor, and what few books RuthAnn owned were ripped apart, their pages strewn around everywhere. All the artwork had been torn from the walls, and CDs lay scattered like abandoned Frisbees.

"Oh, Ruthie, what in the world were they looking for?"

Lindsey scanned the bedroom floor until she found a decorative bulletin board that Ruth-Ann's nieces had made. Covered with tidbits and memorabilia from their high school and college years, the board had made a great place to hide the restaurant keys almost in plain sight. In among concert programs, corsages from their prom dates, and spring break souvenirs hung a small cloth bag in their school colors. Easy to get to, easy to overlook. Lindsey found the board near the bed, the small sack still in place.

She straightened, shoving the keys in her pocket, and let out a long sigh, that tense feeling of vulnerability easing.

"I knew you'd know where they were."

Lindsey screamed as she swung around. A tall man, his face partially covered by a ski mask, blocked the doorway into the living room. His wide, bright blue eyes reflected the light from the kitchen, and Lindsey stepped backward. "You always were a snoopy kid. Now it's your turn to die, July Presley." He lunged for her.

His hand clamped on her left arm, his fingers digging into the muscle. She screamed again, as loud as she could. She lashed out, putting all her strength behind a right cross to his nose. He howled in pain as blood spurted. His grip loosened enough that Lindsey jerked free and sprinted for the door into the kitchen, her ankle no obstacle to freedom. Her shoes skidded on debris on the floor and, off balance, she grabbed the doorframe. She slung her body around it and ducked low. Her attacker's hand swung over her, slamming into the wooden frame. He bellowed, but pushed toward her again.

Lindsey scrambled for the back door, tripping over a chair leg and landing hard on the floor. Her assailant lunged again, but his shoes lost traction on the flour dusting the floor. His arms windmilled as he skated toward the sink. He grabbed the counter and turned, just as the front door crashed open.

"Freeze! Police!"

The man did not hesitate. He pointed at her. "I'll find you!" Then, growling obscenities, he bounded over Lindsey and disappeared through the back door into the dark outside.

Two officers rounded the corner from the living room, guns drawn. Jeff was one of them, and Lindsey saw his eyes widen when he noticed Lindsey on the ground. "Lindsey!"

She pointed out the back door. "He—" Her voice faltered, and she swallowed hard. "How did you—"

Jeff motioned to his partner, who took off out the back door. Jeff knelt by Lindsey. "I was outside the car, stretching my legs, and heard you scream. Are you okay?"

Lindsey gasped for breath. "I think. Just scared."

"No doubt."

"The second guy. It was the second guy."

Jeff froze for a moment. "You sure?"

She swallowed. "Yes. I recognized his voice."

His mouth tightened. "Can you stand?"

She nodded, and clutched his arm, her voice pleading, "Help me."

Jeff put his arm around her and lifted her to her feet. She stumbled, clinging to him, relishing the security of his closeness, his strength. She didn't care how it looked. She didn't want to let go of him. The adrenaline draining from her, she began to shake. "I need to sit down."

He held her tighter. "Can you make it to the front stoop?"

She nodded, and he helped her maneuver through the living room, his arm tight around her. On the stoop, her knees gave way and she sank hard against him. Jeff eased her down onto one of the steps.

"Lindsey, what were you doing in there? This house is a crime scene."

She stared up at him, her hands still shaking. "I know. I just didn't think about that." Lindsey realized that wasn't quite the truth and her voice faltered. "I mean, I did, but I didn't think it would matter. That y'all were through with your work in there. And I just needed to get them before anyone else did!"

"Get what?"

She fumbled in her pocket and pulled out the keys. "My keys. RuthAnn had a set for the diner and one for my house. It didn't occur to me *that's* why the house was ransacked. That's what he was looking for!" She took a deep, quivering breath. "I knew the keys were well hidden, but I just started feeling…I don't know…vulnerable… to have them over here in an unsecured house."

"You should have called us.…" His voice trailed off as his face tightened. "How do you know that's what he was after?"

Lindsey shoved the keys back in her pocket, and crossed her arms across her belly. "That's what he said in there. After I got the keys. He said, 'I knew you'd know where they were.'"

Jeff's voice deepened. "Did he say anything else?"

Tears slid down Lindsey's cheeks. "He said it was my turn to die. That he'd find me." She swallowed hard. "And he called me July."

"July?" Jeff scowled. "Why July?"

"It's the name I grew up with. It changed when I went into foster care after my mother died. I asked my new family to change it, and they helped me make it happen. No one's called me July since then." She grimaced. "Of course, that's why it took so long for June to find me."

Jeff closed his eyes as if a wave of pain had washed over him.

"Jeff?"

He opened his eyes again. "He had to know you as a child." He hesitated, then continued. "I really didn't want this to be about you."

She leaned harder against him. "Neither did I."

"But it is. This isn't about RuthAnn at all. It's about you. His target for all of this is you."

SIX

Standing under a tree in the yard of Lindsey's house, Jeff stared at the three sisters, clustered together on the front steps. The sun had edged up over the horizon, and the golden light created sharp-edged shapes on the lawn. Near him, Sheriff Ray Taylor stood with his chief deputy, Daniel Rivers, who was married to the oldest sister, April.

"I can't believe she went over there in the middle of the night," Daniel muttered. "What was she thinking?"

"How unsafe she felt." Jeff crossed his arms. "With those keys still over there, she talked herself into a panic. She's been alone so long, it never occurs to her to ask for help, even with a cop standing right outside the house. If something's wrong, you fix it yourself."

Ray cleared his throat. "It's not just Lindsey. They all think like that, even after they get married." He, too, watched the three women, although his eyes were mainly on his wife, June.

"No kidding." Jeff turned to look at his boss. "When I told Lindsey she couldn't open the diner for breakfast, she called someone and made arrangements for it to happen. I think June and April are going over there when they're done here."

Ray nodded. "They should. People talk to June. They may hear something from the locals. No sign of the assailant?"

Jeff shook his head. "No, sir. The foot chase ended when the suspect took off in a small, dark-colored sedan. Toyota or maybe a Honda. No lights, no license plate."

Ray rested one hand on his pistol grip. "Probably stolen anyway. My guess is it's in a ditch somewhere under ten feet of garbage or over in Fred's quarry under twenty feet of water. What are your plans for the day?"

Jeff glanced back at Lindsey. "In-depth interview. She said she couldn't sleep because she dreamed about the GTO. There's something there from her past, but she can't get to it. Plus, the trace we started yesterday on the GTO should be back. Then I plan to check on the guy in the hospital."

"Fine, but that boy's in a coma. Don't spend a

lot of time there. You focus on Lindsey. Whatever's going on, she's at the heart of it."

"Yes, sir."

"And Gage?"

Jeff looked at Ray.

"Keep her alive."

Jeff nodded curtly and the other two men left. Taking a deep breath, Jeff walked to the women, who stopped muttering among themselves and looked up at him.

June stood up. "We've come up with a plan to keep my sister safe and away from this maniac."

Whatever Jeff had planned to say went right out of his head. "I'm sorry. What did you say?"

"Well, since y'all can't seem to keep her safe—"

"Now, wait a minute, she—"

"—we've decided she should move in with April and Daniel. Daniel will be there when he's not on duty, and they have an alarm system. And Polly."

Jeff stared. "Polly…"

April spoke up, her voice only slightly milder than June's. "You know, Aunt Suke's German shepherd."

"I know who Polly is."

April stood. "Aunt Suke isn't feeling well right

now, so she's staying with us. And Polly. And you know no one messes with Polly."

"Obviously, this house isn't safe, even with y'all standing guard at night." June stepped closer to him. "And y'all can't keep that up for long. The department's just not that big. You'll wear everyone out."

Jeff looked behind him, but the respective husbands of Lindsey's sisters had vanished. "Cowards," Jeff muttered under his breath. He turned back, focusing on Lindsey, who'd been watching her sisters as if she were at a tennis match. "What about you? Are you on board with this?"

Lindsey, who'd been almost buoyant and determined at the first fight, now looked pale and defeated, which made Jeff's chest ache. She shrugged one shoulder. "I don't like it. They live over in Caralinda. It adds another twenty minutes to the drive to the diner. But they make sense, about having people around. It probably would be safer." She motioned to her front door. "We already know this isn't exactly the securest place…"

Jeff squatted to put himself eye level with her. "And?"

Taking a deep breath, she pushed her sleeve up. A hand-shaped bruise had already formed on her biceps, the finger marks distinct on her skin. Jeff caught his breath as she whispered, "He's really strong. Stronger than the kid was. Stronger than I've ever—"

"He's a monster," June declared. "Let us help you keep her safe."

Jeff stood up. "So what's your plan?"

June blinked twice, almost as if his acquiescence caught her off guard. But not for long. She motioned at April. "We know how this works. You need to talk to her at length. You've already made that clear. In the meantime, April and I will pack up most of the essential stuff here and move it to April's place. Then we'll go to the restaurant. We'll focus on keeping it up and running while y'all solve this thing." She paused only a brief second. "And you have to. If this dates back to something from our childhood, this is going to be bad for all of us. You have to get this monster out of our lives. *All* our lives. Deal?"

"Deal."

They looked down at Lindsey, who smiled wanly and nodded. "Deal." She pulled the keys out of her pants pocket. "You'll need these. And don't forget the stuff on the bedside table."

April patted her shoulder. "We won't. I'll see you tonight." She motioned toward June, and the two older Presley sisters went inside the house.

Jeff sat down on the step next to Lindsey. "You're *really* all right with this?"

"June *can* be overbearing."

"Understatement."

Lindsey laughed, which made Jeff relax a bit. "True. But she means well. And she makes sense. I might sleep better with April and Daniel in the house."

"Not to mention the smartest German shepherd in three counties."

She nodded, looking weary again. "So…let's get on with it."

"You need your crutch?"

Lindsey shook her head. "Not if you don't mind my leaning on your arm."

"Not at all." He offered it to her, and she grasped his forearm, pulling herself to her feet. They moved slowly toward his car, Lindsey clinging to him the entire time.

No, he thought, I don't mind at all.

The ride back to the station started quietly, with Lindsey leaning against the passenger door, staring out as the day grew brighter and warmer. The light through the trees flashed across her face as Jeff drove to the station in Bell's Springs. Jeff fought the urge to reach out and stroke her arm, find some way to comfort her. But everything he thought of seemed awkward. He had never been good in such a situation.

About halfway there, Lindsey broke the silence with a sigh. "I thought I could handle him, the way I always handled my father. I didn't realize...I failed at something I thought I had conquered. I feel like such a wimp."

Jeff struggled for the right words. "But you aren't. You were under a lot of duress at the wreck. Not a good time for judgments about someone's size or strength."

Lindsey smiled shyly. "Is sounding like a cop your default mode of conversation?"

Jeff felt his face heating up. "Yeah, I guess. It's what I know."

She nodded and leaned her head back against the seat. "I think we all do that. I'll sometimes fall back on restaurant jargon."

"What do you mean—like you handled your father?"

Lindsey looked down at her hands a few moments, as if weighing her thoughts. "You know about my dad, right?"

Jeff nodded, then shrugged. "I know from April and June that he was abusive."

"That's the polite term. He was a drunken lout who pounded on all of us. The only reason he stayed out of jail as long as he did was that the police couldn't prove anything. They knew what went on in that house, and they really tried. He would go nuts, and they'd take him to jail for abuse or public drunkenness and resisting arrest. But without my mother's testimony… He didn't go to prison until after…" She crossed her arms and took a deep, steadying breath. "Until after he killed my mother and my brother. Until then… I was still pretty young. And when you're a kid, your dad is big to you. A hulk."

Jeff remembered how big he'd thought his own dad was. "Huge."

"Truth was, my dad was only about five-eight. I didn't realize that until I was older. Not a big guy, but wiry. Mama was about my size, maybe a little bigger." She shook her head slowly. "But this guy was taller than you." She squinted at him. "How tall are you?"

"Six-two or so."

She nodded, staring at him, clearly making the comparison in her mind. "Yeah, so he's six-four maybe. Two hundred twenty pounds, at least. Maybe two fifty. And strong." She rubbed her arm gently. "No one—not my dad or anyone from my time on the streets—has grabbed me like that. I thought he was going to rip my arm off."

"But you fought back well. You bloodied him."

Again, she shrugged one shoulder, then fell silent, looking out the window again.

"We'll find him, Lindsey. We'll stop this. You have to believe that."

"I do," she said, her voice a bare whisper. "But I'm also beginning to understand my mother's fear. Why she didn't…" Slowly, almost absently, she began drawing circles and lines on the window.

Jeff suddenly found it hard to swallow. Never before had he wanted so badly to hold her, assure her that everything would work out. He had admired Lindsey's strength and courage for so long that her sudden vulnerability cracked something inside that threatened to overwhelm him. It took all the professionalism he could muster to stay silent and keep driving.

Eventually, Jeff pulled up in front of the converted storefront that served as the Bell County Sheriff's Department. He helped Lindsey out of the car and, at Ray's suggestion, put her in the conference room instead of an interrogation room. The leather chairs of the conference room made a better resting place for her battered body, and she could elevate her ankle.

As he brought in a digital recorder and the paperwork he needed, he saw that Lindsey had grabbed a piece of paper and started to sketch.

He sank down in a chair, watching her, fascinated by this unexpected talent.

"He has reddish hair," she murmured.

Jeff snapped to attention and scrambled to turn on the recorder. "Say that again."

She continued to sketch. "Sitting here, and in the car, I kept going over and over the attack in my mind, trying to remember as much as I could. And details kept coming back, as if I was seeing everything in slow motion." She shuddered, reliving the moment, then took a deep, calming breath.

"He wore a ski mask that covered his face, but the eyeholes were stretched, showing some of his forehead. When he came at me, something about him didn't look right. But in the heat of the attack, it didn't occur to me why that was. Just now it came to me. His eyes looked…bare. It was like he didn't have any eyebrows. But I think they were there, just very light. He didn't seem to have any eyelashes, either, which would be consistent with him being a reddish-blond. Redheads and blonds sometimes have eyelashes and eyebrows so light they seem to disappear."

She moved the pencil down to fill out the sketch around his eyes. "His eyes were blue, but darker than the average blond's, almost sapphire." She continued drawing the outline of his face.

"The mask was pretty tight and it outlined his jaw." She hesitated, looking at the overall drawing, then handed it to him. "The nose is probably not right at all. With that coloring and jawline, he's probably from Germanic stock, Anglo-Saxon. But that's the best I can do."

Jeff's eyebrows arched as he stared at the drawing. "This is great. More than most people can recall."

"We all did something to escape. April read. June got into trouble. I drew. I refined my observation skills in culinary school, where you need to walk into a kitchen and immediately know if anything is out of whack with the staff. You become exceptionally observant when you're in charge of a kitchen or you don't survive. I used to go home at night and sketch the last scene in the kitchen, just to see if I could see something that could be done better."

"You're a woman of many talents."

She smiled weakly. "Thanks."

He stood. "Be right back. I want to get this out to the patrol officers." He stepped into the bullpen and gave the drawing to an officer to scan and distribute. Returning to the conference room, he settled in a chair facing her. "Now for the rough stuff."

Lindsey nodded and stiffened her back. "Let's do it."

Jeff picked up his pen, poised to take notes, then he looked directly into her eyes. "Let's start with your dream. Tell me every detail you remember."

Lindsey hesitated, and Jeff saw the reluctance in her eyes. She blinked and her mouth tightened. In her lap, her fingers twisted around each other. He leaned a little closer to her, relying on his experience with other victims, other adults who had been abused as children. "Lindsey, I know you want to do this…but you don't. You've overcome so much that you feel invaded this time, as if all the things you've put behind you have come rushing back to haunt you. I know you're in pain as few other folks can understand.

"But everything that you've been through can help us catch this guy. Even your dreams. Because your mind knows things you may not realize on the surface. I can't promise this will always be private information, but for now, it's between you and me."

Her eyes widened during his speech, and her fingers stilled. "I trust you," she whispered.

He leaned back, oddly honored by her words. "I'll do my best to take care of you."

"I know." She thought for a few more moments,

then nodded, almost to herself. "I dreamed about my mother at first. I'd been reading in her diary before I went to sleep, and I guess that led to the dream."

"Why were you reading her diary?"

"I read it every night. It's a way of staying close to her, getting to know her in a way I couldn't when she was alive. I was so young." She paused, blinked hard, then continued. "After she died, my father went to prison on a life sentence, and I went into foster care. Before I did, the people who cleaned out our house let me take just a few things with me, and I took my mother's music box. She loved it so much. Only later did I find the diary in a secret compartment in the bottom. It was like discovering her all over again."

Lindsey shifted, tucking her good foot beneath her and hunching forward like a small child. "When I had that flash of memory of my father at the wreck, his face was all beat up, all cut and bloody. It's confusing because my father was always the aggressor. I can only remember one time when he got beat up, and Mama wrote about it in the last entry in her diary." Tears slipped down Lindsey's cheeks again.

Jeff paused and picked a box of tissues from a credenza against the wall. He pushed them toward Lindsey, who grabbed one, a fleeting smile of thanks crossing her face. She wiped her face, then balled the tissue into one palm.

"What happened that day?" Jeff asked quietly.

Lindsey shrugged and looked down at her hands. "I don't know. Mama didn't see what happened—just the aftereffects. She thinks I saw something, but I don't remember. I don't even remember that day. That whole period of my childhood just blurs into one long stretch of fear and pain."

"That's probably your mind working to protect you. You were just a kid."

Her mouth twisted. "Maybe. But this part would be easier if my memories weren't blocked."

Jeff paused and leaned closer to her, placing one hand on Lindsey's arm. He lowered his voice, keeping the tone low and soothing. "Do me a favor. Close your eyes and let the dream come back to you."

She did. "Okay."

"How did your mother appear in the dream?"

Lindsey sighed. "Beautiful. Perfect. Unhurt."

"What did she have on?"

"She wore her favorite jeans and a big, comfy flannel shirt, as if she'd been working in the yard. She loved working in the yard. Had such a green thumb. She motioned me to follow her, and we went down a forest path. So pretty! Little flowers lined the way. I could see all this detail in them."

"Can you smell them?"

A gentle smile lit her face. "Sweet. Like strawberries."

"Are you lost?"

She shook her head. "No. Mama seems to know where we're going. She keeps smiling and pulling me along."

"How do you feel about that?"

"Curious. Excited."

"Where does it lead?"

"A meadow. Really bright. Lots of grass, but the wind is blowing. RuthAnn's there, holding my keys up, like she's teasing me with them. You know…kinda like, 'Here they are, come and get them.'"

"Do you get them?"

"No. I start to, then all of a sudden, everything goes dark…then there's a spotlight on RuthAnn. Only suddenly it's not a spotlight, it's headlights. Then that GTO comes out of nowhere, heading straight for her. I scream for her to get out of the way, and that's when I woke up."

Lindsey stirred and opened her eyes, but Jeff tightened his grip slightly. "Not yet. Stay there for a minute."

She closed her eyes again.

"I know you were afraid. What else?"

"Yes. I just want to get away, get RuthAnn away."

"Did you see who drove the car?"

Lindsey shook her head. "The windows are black."

"Did you see who beat up your father?"

"Karen's husband."

Lindsey's eyes shot open, and she stared at him. Her lips parted but no sound came out.

"Are you all right?"

She hesitated, then nodded. She gasped. "How did you do that?"

Jeff released her arm and leaned back. "I didn't. You did. Lindsey, your memories aren't blocked. They're blurry so you can tuck them away and get on with your life. But they are there. Do you know who Karen is? Or her husband?"

"Not a clue. I don't even know why I said that." Her eyes widened. "But June or April might know."

"Take me through the attack one more time."

Lindsey seemed to come back to herself. She sat up, and put her foot on the floor again. She described the attack in RuthAnn's house again, in more vivid detail than she had at the scene. Jeff took notes, but was grateful for the recorded backup. Especially since he couldn't resist watching her as she described the night's events.

Unlike her words about her dream, Lindsey's voice grew stronger and held steady. Her cheeks flushed with anger. The fear the man had instilled in her faded, and the determined entrepreneur he'd come to know returned. She'd been shaken, but not defeated. By the time she reached the point where the man had bolted out the back door, her eyes flashed with the need to find the answers to all this. She paused and took a deep breath, then peered at him closely.

"What?" he asked.

"The boy. He was a blond. You don't think there's a blood connection, do you?"

Jeff made a note. "Could be. Something to check."

"Surely a man wouldn't talk like that about his own son. He said he deserved to die!"

Jeff leaned back in the chair. "He also involved him in kidnapping and attempted murder. Lindsey, I don't think this man shows many of the normal civilities."

"True. When are we going to the hospital?"

"I'm going later this morning. You need to rest. I'll run you over to April's—"

"Work would be better. Even better, I could go with you."

"Lindsey—"

She stopped his words with a hand on his arm. "I know you want to take care of me." She leaned forward, her eyes focusing on his. "I appreciate it. More than you know. And now that most of the adrenaline has worn off, you'd think I'd want to sleep. But I'm still too keyed up. All I would do is pace. In fact, I doubt I'll rest much until this is over. Let me go with you. It might help to see him. Then I need to work. I can bat things around with June and April, and we might even come up with something out of our childhood. I'll rest when this is done."

Jeff hesitated. The warmth of her hand on his arm was reassuring, almost comforting, but his misgivings about her being out in the open, even at the restaurant, ran deep. And she did need rest. A lot of it. Her eyes, as intent as they were on him, were darkly shadowed, her cheeks drawn. The investigator in him, however, knew that a visit with her attacker and an afternoon with her sisters might be just what it took to loosen Lindsey's memory.

Jeff relented with a deep exhale. "All right." He leaned forward and put his hand over hers. "I'll take you with me. But promise me you'll stay alert and aware of everyone around you. I don't know what I'd do if anything happened to you."

SEVEN

Through the windows of the ICU, Jeff watched the nurses care for the man who'd kidnapped Lindsey, wishing he felt more anger, more satisfaction that the man suffered for his crimes. *It's what I should be feeling, right?* Instead, the investigator in him was filled with curiosity. *Why did you do this? Were you part of the plan or a dupe who didn't know what you were getting into?*

Lindsey never said the man had tried to kill her; just deliver her.

Beside him, Lindsey remained as silent as she had since they'd arrived. On the drive down, they had talked again about the accident, but nothing new stood out from their conversation. Jeff continued to hold back the information about the switchblade. It was a street knife, one for up close and personal contact. Lindsey showed a lot of confidence and strength following such trauma, but there had been too many moments of doubt, of lingering fear. He wanted her to be wary, not completely terrified.

"I wish they would tell us something," Lindsey whispered. "Do you think he's going to die?"

They had talked to the doctor, who couldn't tell him much about the man's condition, citing the privacy laws. But in the hour or so they had watched the nurses come and go, checking the man's vitals and levels of medication, Jeff had seen no expectation at all that the man would awaken from his coma when they entered. He'd asked one if the man's condition had changed, only to receive a curt shake of the head in response.

"Officer? Miss?"

They turned and Jeff looked down at the charge nurse, who was holding a clipboard. Jeff stood at least a foot taller and was both heavier and younger, but he'd watched her give orders and had no doubt she could put him in his place. "Yes, ma'am?"

"Am I to assume this young man will be arrested?"

"Yes, ma'am. He more or less already is. We have his prints. He'll be formally booked if he wakes up."

She gave a sharp nod. "*If* he wakes up."

Lindsey gasped but remained silent. She

turned back to stare at the young man behind the glass.

The nurse went on. "We're still holding his personal effects, knowing they would be considered evidence in a crime. Will you sign for them?" She held out the clipboard toward him.

Jeff straightened, trying to fight a surge of eagerness, as he took a pen from her. "Absolutely. Has anyone else inquired about him?"

"Not here. Someone might have called in, but the patient information operator wouldn't have given out anything on the phone. Family have to be given a code in order to inquire."

"Thanks. By the way, you said, '*If* he wakes up.' You don't think he will?"

She checked his signature, then peered at him over her reading glasses. The shadows around her eyes told of long shifts and distraught relatives, but the blue of her eyes glistened with awareness. "I can't give you a medical opinion. You know that."

"Yes, ma'am. Wasn't asking for one. I was inquiring about your…experience in these sorts of things."

She continued to stare at him a few moments. Finally, she took her glasses off and nodded toward the sack in his hands. "I'd suggest you do what you can with his effects, in the way of evidence. I doubt a confession will be forthcoming. Clear enough?"

"Yes, ma'am."

"Good. Which means there's no reason for y'all to linger, clogging up the walkways. Shoo."

Her last word, uttered with more affection than command, made Jeff smile. He tipped his head at her, then looked down at Lindsey. "You ready to go?"

She hesitated. "Do you think we'll ever know why he did it?"

"Probably not."

Lindsey glanced up at him, her eyes bright with unshed tears. "Seriously?"

"Seriously." He touched her arm. "Lindsey, that can be one of the most frustrating parts of my job. Sometimes you have solutions but no reasons. We know that he kidnapped you, but we think he did it for someone else. We may find the connection, we may find out why they kidnapped you. But if he dies, we'll most likely never know *why* he chose to, or had to, do it."

She looked back at the boy. "That stinks."

"Yes."

She stared through the glass a few more moments, then straightened her shoulders. "Okay, let's go."

"Did you remember anything else?"

She shook her head. "No. I was praying for him."

They headed out, Jeff cradling the sack under one arm as Lindsey leaned heavily on the other. She still limped, but moved much better than she had last night. As soon as they emerged from the hospital, his cell phone buzzed. When he opened it, Ray Taylor barked in his ear.

"Gage! Where are you?"

"The hospital. We—"

"Get back up here as soon as you can. We found RuthAnn's car. Troy's headed over to haul it out of the quarry right now."

Jeff's gut tightened. "RuthAnn?"

Lindsey clutched his arm tightly. "Did they find her?"

Ray continued. "Not sure if RuthAnn is in the car yet. Fred said one of the divers found it. It's about twenty, maybe twenty-five feet under water. The diver who found it is going to help Troy hook it up. Just get here as soon as you can."

When he ended the call, he noticed that Lindsey's face was pale with anxiety. "Did they find her?" she asked.

Jeff shook his head. "Her car. We have to get back."

The drive out of Nashville never felt so long, even with his blue lights flashing to clear the way of his well-over-the-speed-limit run up the interstate back to Bell County. He skidded into the quarry, and drove down a long gravel ramp to the edge of the water that had long ago flooded the abandoned quarry. About fifty yards in front of them, Troy's largest tow truck had a small foreign car dangling from a cable, grill down, over the quarry. Water poured out of the vehicle, back into the quarry and onto the gravel shore as Troy moved it slowly over land.

Before he could stop her, Lindsey was out of the car, half running, half limping toward the cluster of people who had gathered to watch the spectacle.

Jeff followed. "Lindsey, wait!"

She didn't. "I have to see!"

Ray saw her coming and blocked her path. She fought against him, trying to push past him. Jeff ran toward them, Lindsey's desperate words reaching his ears.

"I have to see! Ray, I have to!"

"Lindsey!"

She whirled, and Jeff started at the distress on her tear-streaked face. "I have to see, Jeff! I don't want anyone else to die! Please!"

"No, Lindsey, you don't want to see this."

She lunged toward him and he grabbed both her arms. "Please! I have to see if I got her killed!"

He pulled her close. "Listen to me. *Listen!*" She grew still, and he dropped his voice as low as he could in the presence of the noisy tow operation. "*You* did not do anything. No matter what we find out, this is *not* your fault. Never, *ever* think that, you hear me? No matter what anyone says to you, this isn't your fault. And if RuthAnn is in that car, you do *not* want to see her. You have good memories of her, great memories of working with her. If she's there, she's dead, and you can't change that. She will have been in the water for hours, and that's not something anyone who cared about her should see. You don't want that image in your mind."

Lindsey didn't move for a few moments, her breathing labored. "This wouldn't have happened if not for me."

"You don't know that. Don't let anyone convince you otherwise."

Ray, who had been hovering nearby, spoke coldly. "Listen to him, Lindsey. No matter what *anyone* told you."

Ray's words sparked Jeff's curiosity, but he focused on Lindsey. "Lindsey, you're the victim in this. This isn't happening because of you. It's happening because some psycho is out of control. That's not your doing. It's his."

Slowly, the tension ebbed out of Lindsey's

body and she straightened up. She nodded, and placed her hands over his, pushing him away. She swallowed hard. "I know. But you tell me. Okay?"

He nodded, stroking her shoulder. "We're in this together. I'm right here. I'll take care of you."

Behind them, Troy lowered the car to the gravel at the edge of the quarry with a sickening crunching noise. Fred, the quarry's manager, and a number of sport divers who used the flooded quarry for training and practice dives moved steadily backward from the car, their faces somber, their eyes curious. Water continued to flow out of the small car as it settled awkwardly on the gravel.

Ray approached it slowly, as Troy shut down the towing operation and began removing the chains and hooks from the car. Another gush surged forth when Ray opened the door. Stepping back until the torrent subsided, Ray peered into the car, into the backseat, then the front. Turning to Jeff, he shook his head. Pulling on a pair of latex gloves, Ray then motioned to an officer standing nearby. The young officer popped the lock on the car's trunk and lifted the lid. Both of them looked in.

Lindsey backed into Jeff, who grabbed her

shoulders, steadying her. "She's in there, isn't she?" Lindsey whispered.

But, again, Ray shook his head. Jeff stepped in front of her. "Stay here." Then he trotted over to the wreckage. Ray prowled around the debris in the trunk, which to Jeff looked mostly like old clothes. The entire wreckage smelled like mold and dead fish.

"Anything?" he asked.

Digging through the wet fabric, Ray spotted a leather strap. Tugging hard, he pulled a small leather bag free. He smeared away clinging tags of fabric and algae and unzipped the bag. "Right," he muttered as he lifted out a revolver.

"Spent shells?" Jeff asked.

Ray popped the cylinder free and checked it. "Two. Four unused."

"Apparently, he didn't need them."

Ray snapped the cylinder back into place. "RuthAnn may not be here…"

Jeff finished. "…but she's not coming back."

"I don't know what I'd do if anything happened to you."

"I'm right here. I'll take care of you."

Jeff's words echoed in Lindsey's mind. The caring look on his face and the intensity of his voice made her chest tighten and almost took her breath away. She knew that the events of the last two days had pushed them closer, but his declarations had caught her off guard. She wanted to push back, to tell him that she just was not ready for anything more.

Yet she didn't. The words never came to mind when she needed to say them. She also thought back to the unexpected and impulsive invitation she'd issued for a grilled cheese. *What's happening to me?*

"Lindsey?" June bent her head and peered closer at her sister. "You all right?"

Lindsey started and looked up, blinking. The buzz of the customers' conversation hovered in the background of the restaurant.

June's brows furrowed. "Are you sure you don't need to go to April's and rest?"

Behind June, April paused, a pan of fresh biscuits in one hand, the other pressed hard in the small of her back. "Seriously, Lindsey, you look drained. I'm sure the officer outside would be glad to take you over to the house. Your stuff is already in the guestroom, and—"

Lindsey slipped off the stool where she'd perched to make a batch of chicken salad. "No, I'm fine. Really. I just got…distracted. That's all."

And she'd been distracted ever since Jeff had

dropped her at the diner. They'd left the quarry, sharing few words. The implications of finding RuthAnn's car hovered over both of them. Lindsey had entered the back door of the restaurant, locking it behind her, and had taken up residence on a stool near her worktable, hoping chicken salad would keep her mind occupied. It hadn't.

"That distraction wouldn't happen to be dark-haired, about six-two, would he?" April teased, as she wiped one hand on the apron she wore over her jeans and oversize T-shirt. Flour smeared on the front of it, and an unruly strand of strawberry-blond hair slipped from beneath her headscarf.

"Yeah. Kinda lanky for my taste, but I hear he's quite the gentleman." June's voice held a gentle tease, but Lindsey didn't feel up to her sisters' ribbing.

Lindsey opened the fridge and pulled out grapes to add to the salad. "Please don't do this right now." Lindsey noticed the look that April and June exchanged, but ignored it. "I really need to focus on other stuff."

Another look, and June set down the pan of beans she had been holding. "You mean like the fact that someone is trying to kill you?"

Lindsey shrugged one shoulder as she limped back to the table and perched on the stool again.

Her mind felt numb, and weariness plagued every muscle. "Can we just work?"

"Doubt it." June took the grapes from her and pushed the chicken salad back. She wiped her hands on her apron. Then, bracing herself against the table, June hoisted her own petite frame up, sitting where the salad had been a moment ago. She took both Lindsey's hands in hers as April joined them.

"Look, little sister, you're not in this world by yourself anymore. We both know what it's like to hit the streets and make it on your own. We know what it does to your mind. But you're back in a family now, and surrounded by folks you can really trust, like Ray and Daniel and even Mr. Lanky. I know how much you rely on God, and He's still there at your back. We'll try to give you space, but we're also going to fight with you and for you. But you have to help us out, too."

Lindsey looked from June to April, amazement setting in. Since she'd been back, her sisters had been fun and supportive, but in a "life is good and without problems" kind of way. After being away for so long, she had no idea that they'd want to stand with her against a killer. "I don't want you to get hurt. I just found you again."

April's eyebrows arched. "Like we haven't

been before. Like we didn't grow up with a man who could have killed us at any time."

"This guy is a lot bigger and meaner than Daddy was."

June slid off the counter, slivers of her brown hair escaping her headscarf. "No matter. You're not facing this alone. So get used to it."

Lindsey pulled both of them into a tight hug, leaning heavily on June's shoulder. "And this may date back to that time."

Her sisters leaned back, their faces pinched with curiosity. "What do you mean?" asked June.

Lindsey explained what her attacker had said during the fight, her dream, the diary and what Jeff had drawn out of her. "Do either of you know who Karen is? Or her husband?"

April shook her head. "Never heard of her, and I thought I knew everyone in the neighborhood." She glanced through the service window into the dining area. "I need to check the tables. Don't say too much without me."

She headed out, and the din from the tables increased as she began to circulate with a fresh pot of coffee. June picked up the beans and put them in the warming oven. "You know, I may be able to help with the GTO. I talked to Troy, over at the garage, and he said it was a beauty, mostly original parts, but some had been replaced."

"Jeff is tracing the title. They found that and a book in the glove compartment."

"Yeah, but he may not get too far with that title. My guess is it's been scrubbed."

"Scrubbed?"

"Cleaned and reissued." June paused and cleared her throat. "Back in my more, um, troubled days, I used to help a car theft ring in Nashville clean the titles of the ones they stole." She stopped and shook her head, as if to banish a bad memory. "Never mind how. The point is that if—or when—the title dead-ends, he might be able to trace some of the replacement parts. Wichita is the best place for classic GTO replacement parts, and I know some of the dealers there. I could get their info to him. They tend to be pretty persnickety about who they talk to, for a lot of reasons."

"How would that help, if the title has been cleaned and transferred?"

"Shipping addresses. Most folks don't actually travel to Wichita to get the parts. They have them shipped. So even if the title trace goes cold, the parts dealer could easily have a shipping address." She checked the dining room with a quick glance. "You mentioned a book in the car. What book did they find?"

Lindsey shrugged. "An old copy of *Catcher*

in the Rye. Looked like it had been waterlogged at one time. It was all beat up and wrinkled."

June grew still, her eyes narrowing. "*Catcher in the Rye?* For real?"

Lindsey studied her sister. "Yes. Why?"

April poked her head through the service window. "June, get out here. The coffee is getting low." She looked at Lindsey. "Get back to that chicken salad. We have two new orders for it. And put your thinking cap on for new employees."

Lindsey scowled. "Where are the Schneiders?"

June headed toward the door. "They called earlier. Their mom needs their car until noon. They'll be in after that. But we've been buzzing. You need more than two people running this place, especially if your business keeps growing."

"June, what about the book?"

June waved a hand in dismissal. "Probably nothing. I'll tell you later." She disappeared into the dining area and the noise increased even more.

Lindsey grabbed the grapes and started slicing them in half, her scowl deepening. She didn't really want to hire extra people—not yet—but she couldn't keep asking April and June to fill in, with RuthAnn gone and her injured. They had lives—busy ones—that didn't include working here.

Tomorrow. Surely they'll find RuthAnn tomorrow. Or, better yet, she'll call and say she just took a vacation and the burglary happened after she left. Or maybe she managed to escape from some monster... The knife slashed through grapes with increasing speed. Lindsey refused to consider the obvious and most immediate assumption about RuthAnn—that she would never be back.

"It's just wrong," she muttered, "to hire someone to replace her so soon." But if June was right about how the business seemed to be picking up...

"I'd hate to be a grape right now."

Lindsey yelped, bounced off the stool and spun around, knife held at the ready. Her heart thudded, and her breath stopped as she faced the new arrival in her kitchen.

Max Carpenter took a step backward, hands up, face white. "Oh, Lindsey, I'm sorry. I thought you heard me come in."

Lindsey stared at him, her breath caught in her chest, not quite believing it was just Max standing before her. Fear froze her in place for a moment.

"Obviously not," she whispered, still not able to breathe properly.

He lowered his hands. "I'm really sorry."

The drone of the dining room seemed to fade as the buzzing in her own ears increased. "I thought…"

Max stepped forward and eased the knife from her grip. "Breathe, Lindsey. You're still holding your breath." He placed the knife on the counter.

Lindsey stared at him, her hands still raised in a protective posture. "I thought the back door was locked." She gasped in a good breath. "I know I locked it."

Max shook his head slowly, peering at her through the thick lenses of his glasses. "It wasn't locked. It wasn't even latched. I knocked, but I guess you didn't hear me over the folks in there."

Lindsey shook her head, still wary even as the fear eased away. She glanced toward the back of the kitchen. The door where she accepted deliveries and where her employees came and went was down a short hallway that also held the small office for the restaurant. She knew she'd locked it. Double-checked it even. *So who had opened it?*

"Don't worry. I closed and locked it."

She looked back at Max. "Why are you here, Max?"

He stepped away, glancing around the kitchen

nervously. "I came to see if you needed anything. And if you'd heard anything from RuthAnn. I heard about your, um, incident at RuthAnn's last night—"

Lindsey snapped to attention. "How did you hear about that?"

Max ran one hand through his black hair. "Went over to see if I could start cleaning up RuthAnn's house. The officer wouldn't let me in. Said it had become a crime scene all over again. You know nothing in this town remains secret for too long."

Lindsey let out a long sigh. "I know. And, no, we haven't heard anything from RuthAnn."

Max's face scrunched in a puzzled look. "Really? I heard this morning that they found her car in the old quarry that's flooded. Twenty feet under water."

Lindsey nodded, the adrenaline of the fright easing away. "But it was empty. Almost as if it had been stolen and dumped."

The puzzlement on Max's face deepened. "Empty. Really? That's odd." He looked away and his eyes narrowed, as if he were trying to figure something out.

Lindsey stared at him. "Why is it odd?"

He shrugged. "Well, I'm no criminal, but why

would you dump a perfectly good car if it weren't to hide evidence or a body?"

The casual callousness of his comment appalled Lindsey. "Max, we're talking about Ruth-Ann here! Your tenant and my friend! She's not evidence and she's not just a body to be dumped!" Tears stung her eyes, and she slapped her hand on the table. *No! I will not break down. Not now!*

Max jumped. "I'm sorry. I just came to see if I could help."

"Yes!" June shouted through the window. "Max, grab a tray and get out here and bus tables." She pointed at the chopped grapes, then Lindsey. "Mix now. Cry later." She disappeared again.

Silently, Lindsey pointed at the stack of trays they used for bussing. Max grabbed one and disappeared into the dining area. Lindsey grabbed the bowl of chicken salad and began to fold in the chopped grapes, sniffing back any semblance of tears. Leave it to June to command even her tears.

Lindsey grabbed two plates and pulled down a bag of croissants. She was spooning out the salad, when she felt a tickle on her calf and looked down. The neighborhood cat looked up at her and meowed.

"Tulip! What are you doing in here?" Moving smoothly, Lindsey scooped up the cat and headed to the back door, scolding her. "You can't be in here. You have no idea what kind of trouble you'd get me in."

Lindsey entered the hallway and stopped cold. The back door to the restaurant stood wide open.

EIGHT

By the time Jeff picked her up that evening, exhaustion so consumed Lindsey that she almost fell asleep in his car. They said little on the way to April and Daniel's. She skipped supper and settled into one of the guestrooms upstairs. The room's elaborate and comfy decorations closed around her, and the heavy four-poster bed felt safe and secure, but Lindsey barely noticed her surroundings. She dropped into a dreamless sleep, exhausted from the day's drama.

Waking just before her alarm, she padded awkwardly through the rambling antebellum mansion into the industrial-size kitchen to make a cup of tea. Darkness still cloaked the house, but April had scattered night-lights throughout, their dim light providing a clear path. Lindsey's hip and ankle were still sore, but this morning she felt more rested than she had in days. Pushing through the swinging door into the kitchen, she stopped, blinking in bright light. Every light in the kitchen glared, vanquishing all darkness.

"Good morning. You must be Lindsey."

Lindsey blinked again, looking at the older woman sitting at the scarred wooden table. Her long, gray hair cascaded over her shoulders, the strands beside her face tucked behind her ears. Her hands curled around a heavy porcelain mug. Beside her chair, a white German Shepherd sat, her alert eyes focused on Lindsey.

"You must be Mrs. Stockard."

The woman smiled sweetly. "Aunt Suke. Everyone calls me Aunt Suke. Even those who aren't kin." She dropped her hand to the Shepherd's head. "This is Polly." Nodding toward the stove, she continued. "Kettle's already on. April said you liked tea." Aunt Suke pointed toward one of the dark wood cabinets. "Tea's in there. Sugar, honey and cream are here on the table."

"Thank you." Lindsey picked through the boxes in the cabinet, plucking out a tea bag of English Breakfast blend. "I didn't expect anyone up this early."

"Been an early riser all my life. Leftover from when this was a working farm, I reckon. Did April explain earlier that this was my ancestral home?"

Lindsey poured hot water over her tea bag,

then looked around the large kitchen as it steeped. "Yes. And that you gave it to them as a wedding present."

Aunt Suke nodded. "Daniel's been like a son to me. I have no heirs, and after his father died, we just seemed to adopt each other."

Lindsey smiled. "I do love this kitchen. You could run a nice bed-and-breakfast out of here."

Aunt Suke chuckled. "Been told that before. Thought April might take it on, once the house passed to her, but I think she's content to use it for her jams and jellies business. She doesn't want to overload her schedule anymore. Especially not now."

"But it was your family home. Surely there are relatives somewhere."

Aunt Suke scoffed. "Trifling folks, all of them. None worth passing the time of day with, much less giving them my home. It's been here since before the Civil War, when my great-great-great-granddaddy helped settle Caralinda. They would have had it in shambles in a week. April and Daniel love it. They'll take good care of it." She paused and took a sip of tea, watching Lindsey over the edge of her cup. "And I know what it's like not to have family here."

Lindsey dropped her tea bag in the trash and joined Aunt Suke at the table. She reached for the sugar. "You mean the three Presley sisters moving in with no other family?"

"And Daniel. When his daddy was killed, he didn't have anyone else. Now he has April. And you and June."

"And you."

Aunt Suke shrugged one shoulder. "I've been around since he was a baby. Friends, but not kin." She motioned around the kitchen. "And this place was far too big for me to keep staying here alone. April and I more or less swapped. We fixed up her cottage, and I moved in. Daniel looks after both places." She gestured at Lindsey with her cup. "And your Mr. Gage comes over and helps a lot, too. Quite the carpenter, that one."

Lindsey felt heat building in her cheeks. "He's not *my*—" She stopped as the second part of Aunt Suke's sentence registered on her sleep-addled mind. "He's a carpenter?"

Aunt Suke nodded. "So was his daddy and now his stepdad. The two of them—him and his stepdad—added a second story to their garage for his apartment. They could help you with that new restaurant of yours. Folks kid him about still living with his folks, but that's been a good thing. That family's been through a lot, too."

Despite her reluctance, curiosity about Jeff blossomed in Lindsey. "Like what?"

Aunt Suke leaned back in his chair. "Well, you know his daddy died in the first Gulf War, when Jeff was just a kid."

Lindsey shook her head. "I didn't know."

"Turner. Mickey Turner. If you listen to your customers talk, you may hear something come up about the Turners now and then. They still live down in Ridgetop. Nice folks. Not rich, not poor. Mickey was a carpenter and met Jeff's mother when she had him build some bookshelves for her. She used to work as a nurse up at NorthCrest. Anyway, Mickey didn't come home from the war, so Jeff's mom went back to work, even had to take Jeff with her sometimes. They struggled for a long time, 'til she met Alan Gage during one of her E.R. shifts. They married and he adopted Jeff. Jeff went out to L.A. to be a cop, but then Alan got sick, real sick, with cancer. Then his mother came down with it. Jeff came home, took care of them 'til Alan got back on his feet. They're both still looking out for his mom. Alan beat it, but Elizabeth has had a rougher time. Alan and Jeff—they love to build stuff. Alan organized a barn raising last summer for one of the tobacco farmers who'd lost two firing barns during the floods."

Lindsey curled her fingers around her cup to keep them warm. "What was he like as a kid?"

Aunt Suke smiled broadly. "He was a high school star. Not in the athletic way. That was Daniel. Jeff used his brains. He was…what is it the kids call the brainy ones now?"

Lindsey couldn't quite believe it. "A geek?"

Aunt Suke chuckled. "That's it. Everyone around here thought he'd become a teacher or a professor. Then he ups and joins the LAPD. When he came back, some of the girls around here didn't even recognize him, he'd filled out so nicely. Some who hadn't said a word to him in high school started paying a lot of attention to him."

Lindsey leaned forward. "So he's had a lot of girlfriends?"

"A few, but he really—"

Polly stood up, stiff at attention, looking down the hall toward the front door. She let out a low woof, barely more than a cough.

Aunt Suke stood. "Looks like your ride is here."

Lindsey felt confused as she stood up and took her teacup to the sink. "I don't understand. April is supposed to take me in."

"Oh, I doubt he'll let that happen. Not as long as they think you could be in danger."

As if on cue, the sound of a distinctive knock came from the front door. Polly trotted off in that direction, as Lindsey gasped. "I'm not dressed for work!"

Aunt Suke motioned down the hall. "Scoot. I'll keep him busy. But I'd better answer the door or he's liable to think something's wrong and break it down."

Lindsey half ran, half limped up the stairs, annoyed at herself for getting distracted. Again. This was becoming a habit. In her room, she glanced at the clock as she flung off her robe. "Now we're going to be late," she muttered. "I can't afford to be any more distracted. *Especially* about Jeff. Focus, Lindsey!"

Jeff stared down at Aunt Suke, who stood in the door frame, Polly by her side. "Um, I'm here to take Lindsey to work."

Aunt Suke opened the door wider. "Come in, Jeff. Lindsey will be right down. I'm afraid I sidetracked her over a cup of tea this morning. We were talking about you."

Jeff stopped short in the broad foyer, his heels clipping sharply on the hardwood floor. "Me?"

Aunt Suke took his elbow and steered him toward the front parlor. Polly escorted them, her nails clicking, then going silent as they passed from the wood of the foyer to the deep rugs of the parlor. "Of course. Surely, at your age, you realize that when two or more women get together, one of their favorite topics is men. Plus, you're a much more pleasant topic of conversation than the fact that someone wants to kill her. Especially over tea in the morning. Don't you think?"

Jeff smiled, realizing the method in Aunt Suke's gossip. "Indeed I do. So did you come to any conclusions about me?"

Aunt Suke motioned for him to sit, and he perched on the edge of a chair. The front parlor, formal and elegantly decorated with sumptuous Oriental carpets, Queen Anne furnishings and heavy drapes, made Jeff just a tad nervous. He felt too tall, underdressed in his uniform and klutzy.

"Not yet. We'd really just gotten started. I told her about your family, some of your history." Aunt Suke leaned forward, whisperingly conspiratorially. "Enough to know she blushes nicely when your name comes up, especially where other women are concerned."

Jeff's eyes widened. "Other women? But I haven't—"

Aunt Suke put a finger to her lips. "Shh. Never hurts for a lady to wonder. You can clarify things later."

"Aunt Suke—"

The sound of Lindsey coming down the stairs interrupted them both, and Jeff stood and headed toward her. Without her crutch, Lindsey came down the stairs one at a time, but at a pace that made Jeff increasingly nervous.

"Careful," he muttered.

At the bottom and slightly breathless, she looked up at him with a wry smile. "Sorry. Didn't mean to scare you. I'm still a bit shaky on stairs, but I don't fall."

Aunt Suke cleared her throat. "The front steps here, however, are worn stone. Very uneven. After all, they're more than one hundred years old." She straightened, a determined look on her face. "So I think Jeff should carry you to his car."

Jeff and Lindsey stared at her a moment, then looked at each other. Lindsey looked puzzled and a little disturbed, and Jeff grinned at Aunt Suke. "You're incorrigible."

She smiled brightly. "An advantage of age."

Before Jeff could respond, a rapid thumping sounded over their heads, and April appeared at the top of the stairs, her strawberry-blond curls flouncing. She finished buttoning her blouse as she trotted down the stairs. "Sorry! Sorry! Rough start this morning."

Jeff watched her descend, once again struck by how different the three sisters were. Although Lindsey and June were both petite in frame, June had dark hair and dark eyes, while Lindsey was naturally fair. April, on the other hand, stood almost six feet tall and had an athletic build. Lindsey and June's hair lay soft and silky against their heads, while April's wild mane of strawberry curls flared around her head like fire. Yet all three had facial features so similar that their faces seemed carved from the same mold. The wonderful variety of God, he thought affectionately.

April pulled a ponytail holder from around her wrist and quickly bound her hair at the nape of her neck. "I'm not used to these hours."

Jeff realized that April's face held a strange pallor, even as her nose and lips were bright red. "Are you sick, April?"

She waved off his concern. "Supper didn't agree with me. It's nothing." April turned, looking admiringly at her sister. "Lindsey, I don't know how you do this every day. You'd have to love it."

Lindsey grinned. "I do. But I've always been an early riser, too. So it's not so tough."

Aunt Suke made a shooing motion at them. "Then y'all be off doing what you love. I've got work to do myself."

April gave the older woman a quick hug and a peck on the cheek, then they headed out the door. At the stone steps, Jeff paused and offered Lindsey his arm. "To humor Aunt Suke, mademoiselle?"

She grinned up at him and slipped her hand around his arm. He escorted her to the front seat of his car, then held the back door for April. As they settled in, Lindsey looked at her sister in the mirror. "I thought you said Aunt Suke was sick."

April nodded. "She is, although you'd never know it from talking to her. Her diabetes got out of control last month, and she's still wrestling with it. She had a couple of blackouts, so the doc doesn't want her to live alone right now. They've also run some tests on her heart, and we're waiting for the results."

"When will those come in?"

"Tomorrow."

As Jeff listened to the women chat a few moments, his thoughts went back to RuthAnn's car. After they had sent Lindsey and her sisters back to the restaurant, he and Ray had gone over the wreck with a fine-tooth comb. They'd found nothing. No bullet holes or signs of violence that couldn't be explained by the car going in the quarry. Any human evidence, if there had been any, had been washed away by the algae-laden water. The clothes they'd found looked as if they could be RuthAnn's—petite women's clothes of a style an older woman might wear—but they had no way of knowing for sure. The gun's serial number had been filed off, so they sent it to the TBI lab, along with the knife to see if the forensics folks there could raise the number. Jeff had met one of the lab guys at the Tennessee Bureau of Investigation. He knew they had the talent as well as the technology to raise a number that had been acid-burned, much less one that had been merely filed.

Now the car sat next to the GTO in Troy's garage. He couldn't think of anything else to do to it forensically that could help them with the investigation. So he was left with Lindsey's memory and the GTO. June had sent an email last night about the parts dealers she knew, since—as she'd predicted—the title trace had ended with a fake name and an address that was now under Old Hickory Lake north of Nashville. If he could trace one of the parts to a dealer who would give him a shipping address, then he might be able to use that to jar a memory from—

Lindsey nudged his elbow.

Jeff jerked his arm, caught off guard by her touch. He looked toward her, blinking. "What?"

Both women burst out laughing, and Jeff fought a sudden sense of confusion.

"Where were you?" Lindsey asked.

He shook his head. "I don't understand."

"I've been talking to you for a couple of minutes."

Jeff's cheeks grew hot. "Sorry. I was thinking about the case."

Lindsey perked up. "Anything new?"

"Did June email you last night?" April asked.

Jeff nodded. "She did. After I drop y'all off, I'm going to talk to Troy, see if he has any insight into those replacement parts in the car. It might be better if he contacted June's dealers. More believable coming from another car guy."

April scowled. "You're not staying with us?"

Lindsey's shoulders hunched, and she seemed even smaller as she drew away from him. "You're not leaving us alone at the café, are you?"

Jeff shook his head. "No. Absolutely not. But Ray is convinced this guy will never come around with cops hanging out next to you. He's hired a couple of security guards he knows. They'll be in plain clothes."

April's voice deepened, her words almost a growl. "Doesn't that make Lindsey *bait?*"

Jeff took a deep breath, but Lindsey spoke first. "No. I like it." She looked at April. "I think Ray's right. This guy will never come around with the police nearby. And I don't think he'll try anything in the daytime, in front of people. He may want me dead, but he doesn't want to be caught. He ran out of RuthAnn's house when he could have killed me then. But he thinks no one knows who he is. If there are no officers around, he might just show up to check things out."

"That's pretty much Ray's thinking."

"Well, I *don't* like it. And I don't think June will, either."

Lindsey smiled gently. "You're my sisters. You're not supposed to like it."

April leaned back against the seat and crossed her arms.

As Jeff turned the cruiser into the restaurant drive, however, April's words stuck in his mind. *Doesn't that make Lindsey* bait? He hadn't thought about it from that angle. Ray had made it sound so logical…

Beside him, Lindsey stiffened, staring at the restaurant.

Jeff parked the car. "What's wrong?"

"April," she whispered. "Did we leave the dining-room light on?"

Her sister came alert. "No. I double-checked it myself, right after we set the alarm."

"Look."

They all stared. The light of the restaurant's main dining area glared out into the early-morning darkness. Over the carefully painted name of the Coffee-Time Café, a broad X had been drawn on the window in a smeared, garish red.

NINE

"Stay here." Jeff motioned for Lindsey and April to remain in the car.

"Aren't you going to wait?" Lindsey whispered, her voice choked with fear. He had called for backup as soon as he'd parked the cruiser.

"I'm just going to check the back, in case someone tries to leave."

"Jeff, please—"

"Lock the doors."

Lindsey watched him crouch beside the front wheel, observing the area. He then sprinted for the corner of the diner, which would give him cover from all the windows.

"Blind spot," muttered April. "You need a camera on that spot."

"I need more cameras all over the place," Lindsey replied softly, doing everything she could to fight the fear that made all her muscles tense up. She gripped the dash, her eyes never leaving Jeff as he carefully approached the back corner of the building. From a distance, sirens screeched through the air.

He glanced around the corner, then back. Pausing, he looked again, more slowly, then disappeared around the building.

"I can't just sit here." Lindsey gulped a breath of air and reached for the door handle.

"Lindsey, no!" From the backseat, April began to pound on the protective shield between the front and back seats. "You don't know who's out there."

"I know Jeff's out there." Lindsey opened the door.

The sirens screamed closer as three patrol cars roared into the parking lot, the officers inside piling out in a rush.

"Look, he's there!"

Lindsey turned back, staring at the restaurant. Jeff had returned, gun still drawn, but he looked behind them, and motioned for the other officers to approach. When he saw that Lindsey's door stood open, he scowled, motioning for her to stay put. She closed it reluctantly, and crossed her arms, fear mixing with anger deep inside. "I hate this."

"We all do," muttered April.

They sat, watching officers move about in a formation that seemed random and organized at the same time. Lindsey tried to watch the operation as a whole, but found her gaze constantly seeking out Jeff. *Why not?* she asked herself. *He's a friend.*

But just a friend? She could hear Aunt Suke's words encouraging her, and hear her own reply. *Yes, I don't have time for...*

Jeff's face appeared in the restaurant window, over the ugly blotched paint. When he gave an all-clear signal, Lindsey let out the breath she'd been holding. He opened the front door, and Lindsey and April scrambled out and headed up the steps.

Jeff holstered his pistol. "I don't think anything was touched but the window. The back door was standing open, but it doesn't look forced. Someone either picked it or he has a key."

Lindsey stiffened. "Picked. It had to be picked." *Just like yesterday.*

Jeff hesitated, and Lindsey got the message. "I know. We can't be sure. I'll call a locksmith and have all the locks changed." She started to press by Jeff. "Now we need to get started—"

Jeff blocked her path. "Wait. You can't go in there."

Lindsey stared up at him. "But you said nothing had been disturbed."

"It's still a crime scene. We'll need to process it."

"I open in less than thirty minutes!"

Jeff gaped at her. "Lindsey, you can't open. It's a crime scene."

Lindsey braced her fists on her waist, anger coursing through her. "He's not going to win by putting me out of business! If he didn't disturb anything, then this is exactly what he wanted. To put me out of my place, keep me from doing business. No!"

Jeff stood his ground. "Lindsey, there's no option here."

She opened her mouth to protest, when April's firm but gentle grip tightened on her shoulder. "I have an idea. A compromise." As they both looked at her, she smiled. "How long would it take you to clear the coffee equipment?"

More than two hours later, Jeff paused in his work to peer out the front window at a steady stream of cars flowing through a carefully orchestrated arc in the parking lot. At the top of the arc, April, June and Lindsey greeted customers, explained the situation, and offered them free coffee or tea and a pastry as an apology for the inconvenience. They smoothed over the seriousness of the event, and not a single customer left with a frown or a scowl.

"She's turning a problem into an opportunity," Ray said, standing behind Jeff.

"That's the entrepreneur in her." Jeff felt an unexpected pride, watching Lindsey move about easily, even though she still favored her ankle and bruises dotted her face. "She's remarkable."

"Mmm. Find anything remarkable in here?"

Jeff started, turning quickly to face his boss. "Oh, uh…" He cleared his throat as he scanned the dining room of the restaurant. "Not so much in here. Just the paint on the window and a few drops underneath. Looks pretty generic. There's a circle where he set something down on the floor, about the size of a small can of paint."

He gestured for Ray to follow him into the kitchen. "More so in here." The kitchen, normally warm and smelling like biscuits and bacon this time of morning, felt icy and sterile to Jeff. Their footsteps echoed hollowly on the dark wooden floors. He pointed down the short hallway that led to Lindsey's office and the back door. The door stood open, and a groggy locksmith yawned as he worked on installing a new doorknob and dead-bolt lock.

"That was fast," muttered Ray. "Last time I

needed him to install a lock, it took him two weeks to show up."

"Lindsey's pretty persuasive when she sets her mind to something."

"So I see. What did you find?"

Jeff pointed into the office at the old lock works lying on the desk. "He didn't touch anything in here but the recorder. He deleted last night's footage from the cameras. But he left no prints. No help there. The only clue is that the lock's scarred. The door hadn't been forced, but Lindsey insists none of the keys are missing since she pulled the duplicate set out of Ruth-Ann's house. So I took the lock apart. It's scraped up somewhat inside, like it's been picked or a bad copy of the key had to be jiggled and forced." He plucked a small pick from his kit and pointed at a section of the lock. "See? There are tiny shavings left behind. Not from normal use."

Ray didn't peer too closely. "I'll take your word for it. Is that it? Metal shavings?"

Some of Jeff's enthusiasm waned. "Pretty much. No prints on the door or window. There're a couple of smudges in the paint, like he'd worn gloves. Lindsey said nothing has been moved anywhere in here. Considering how many people come and go through the restaurant on a daily basis, I figured fingerprinting most of the surfaces would be useless."

"Probably right. What's your plan now?"

Jeff's shoulders dropped. "Truth is, we don't have a lot left to go on. Lindsey's memory is still unreliable. Her sisters haven't heard of anyone named Karen. I went through the boy's personal effects last night, logged everything into evidence, but there's nothing there. No wallet or ID, just a pair of jeans and a T-shirt you could buy at any store. I'm going to talk to Troy about the replacement parts on the GTO, see if they'll turn up an address. Are those security guards here yet?"

"Outside. And do me a favor. Talk to Lindsey about hiring some help."

"Missing your wife?"

Ray grinned. "Something like that." Then the grin vanished, and Ray crossed his arms. "They aren't going to say anything because they want to help her out in this. But this is April's busiest season, post-harvest and with her trying to get Christmas mailers out. Daniel told me she's been filling orders until after midnight, then coming to bed exhausted. June's the same way with the grants. Some of her deadlines can't be postponed. We're all burning it at both ends."

"No wonder April ran late this morning."

"And I know it may be hard, given what's happened with RuthAnn. But it would also be better for Lindsey to have more help, especially right now. She's going to drive herself right into the ground, if she's not careful."

Jeff nodded and stripped off his latex gloves, dropping them in his kit. "Will do."

Ray clapped Jeff once on the shoulder and strode off, leaving Jeff alone with the locksmith. Through the back door, Jeff watched Ray check with the one other officer who remained at the scene. As they cleared each area of the restaurant, the other men had returned to their regular duties.

Jeff rolled his shoulders back, suddenly wishing for the resources of a much bigger department. Although he loved being here in Bell County, with its relatively low crime rate and close-knit communities, working with larger departments like the LAPD had spoiled him with their easy access to things that juries these days took for granted, like in-depth forensics results. In truth, forensics seldom *solved* anything; evidence just backed up what the detectives discovered or already knew. Sometimes investigators knew exactly who had committed the crime long before they could put together enough evidence to prove it in court.

Still, it would have been nice to have more officers to help with crime scenes and easier access to labs for DNA and weapons checks. He could run fingerprints at their own station, but that pretty much exhausted the immediate scientific help. He sniffed, hearing his mother's words in his head. *Jeff, we have to make do with what God has provided. If wishes were horses, beggars would ride.*

Right, Mom.

"How much longer, Ralph?"

The locksmith paused in his work. "A few more minutes here, then I'll start on the front door. Lindsey wants the cellar door locks changed, too."

"Lock*s?* I thought there was just the one outside entrance."

Ralph wiped his forehead with one sleeve. "Nah, man. In places this old, there was always a way to access the cellar from inside. All the deliveries go in from the outside. Keeps folks from tromping through the kitchen. Hers is at the back of the storeroom." Ralph motioned with a tool toward a narrow door on the opposite side of the kitchen.

Scowling, Jeff went back to his kit and pulled out gloves again. "Don't touch those till I give you the all clear, okay?"

"You got it, boss," Ralph said, picking up a file.

Snapping on his gloves, Jeff took his kit and went to the door of the storeroom. It still stood slightly ajar, having been cleared earlier by one of the officers. *He probably thought it was a dead-end closet, too.*

Jeff turned on the light. Two shelves filled with restaurant supplies lined the narrow room, and there did not seem to be an exit at the back. He looked again at the door. No signs of damage. No lock. Jeff decided to check both sides for prints later, although he suspected any he found would wind up belonging to someone who worked for the restaurant.

Jeff entered slowly, moving toward the back. A creak made him look behind him. The storeroom door slowly swung shut, as if under its own power. Jeff shook his head. "Spooky old houses."

At the back of the closet, he found that one set of shelves ended more than three feet from the rear wall. In the open space was an ancient plank door held shut by a flip latch that looked as if it had been installed in the 1930s. "Really secure." Jeff wondered why Lindsey hadn't replaced it, then thought about the steel-reinforced lock on the outside cellar door, which was connected to the alarm. Probably didn't think she needed to.

Just as we took it for granted. When the officers who'd swarmed to the scene had surveyed the restaurant upon arrival, they'd double-checked the cellar. The heavy lock had not been tampered with and they'd moved on to the back door, which stood open.

Jeff set the kit down, pulled out his gun and stood to one side before yanking open the cellar door. As he expected, silence. The chilled air rushing out of the cellar felt heavy and carried with it the smell of potatoes, turnips and earth. He reached inside the frame and felt for a light switch. The resulting yellow glow illuminated a short set of steps leading down to a rock-walled room filled with hefty, serviceable shelves. Crates of vegetables lined them, and clusters of garlic and peppers hung from the heavy floor joists of the cellar.

Jeff descended the steps, checked under them quickly, then looked around the room. Only the heavy silence of an underground room greeted him in return. A short distance from the steps, a thin string dangled, and Jeff jerked it, turning on more lights. The room extended quite a way underneath the house, but the food supplies were near the door. Farther back looked like unneeded, little-used equipment. Most of the pieces lay beneath thick blankets of plastic and dust.

Jeff moved among the shelves and the stacks

of discarded gear, letting out a long sigh as he realized there was nothing, and no one, down here. He relaxed, his arm pointing the gun toward the floor. Returning to the rear door, he took out his flashlight and peered closely at it. With the outside lock undisturbed, he expected to find this one equally intact.

Only it wasn't. It was damaged, pry marks lining either side of the steel plate, as if someone had tried to jimmy it open from the inside. Recently.

From the inside. Jeff scowled. "Why would—?"

A scuff sounded behind him.

Jeff snapped alert, too late. He swung around, turning directly into the blow aimed for the side of his head. He glimpsed a blurred image of dark hair and white flesh, then a thousand lights exploded behind his eyes and Jeff dropped to his knees. He fought for consciousness, trying to swing his gun up. Searing pain shot up his wrist as the second blow disarmed him. He barely felt the third one, as blackness swarmed over him.

TEN

Lindsey's feet ached. She massaged the muscles in the small of her back, arching, trying to stretch out the kinks. Her ankle throbbed, swelling painfully inside her shoe.

"Big difference between serving coffee on asphalt and running around on wood, huh?" April said, doing her own stretching.

"No kidding." Lindsey checked her watch. Almost nine. The breakfast traffic had dwindled to the occasional late riser. But they'd done the best they could under the circumstances. They'd served more than two hundred cups of coffee and almost as many pastries. Not great for her bottom line, but she knew it would probably pay off in the long run. She also found out that most people already knew about the kidnapping. They expressed sympathy and promised to give the police information, if they came across any. They would watch for strangers around town. They seemed eager to help.

Life in a small town. Once again, she felt grateful God had led her here.

Lindsey glanced at the front of the restaurant, where Ralph had finished changing the front locks. Now he rocked impatiently from one foot to the other as he chatted with Max, who'd wandered over there a little while ago to see if he could help.

"Why hasn't he started on the cellar?" Lindsey asked.

"Don't think we're the ones to ask," June replied from beside her.

Lindsey looked around, an odd, suspicious feeling growing in her gut. The yellow tape still fluttered across the front of the restaurant, but the last of the uniformed officers had departed about thirty minutes before, leaving only the two security guards, plus Jeff and Ralph on the scene. Lindsey squinted, trying to see Jeff through the front window, to no avail. She looked at the guards, one of whom leaned against the hood of his car, looking obvious and official, like an FBI agent at a college frat party. The other one had been circling the property on a regular basis, making rounds.

"Nothing obvious about those guys," she muttered.

June snorted. "I asked Ray if he hired them

from Central Casting. But I think they're from a reputable company. I think he's going to talk to them about fitting in better with the local folk. Not many neckties in our normal crowd."

"Have either of you seen Jeff?"

Her sisters shook their heads.

"I think it's time to shut this down. Word will spread that we're going to be closed the rest of the day. Let's take everything back inside, see what Jeff has found."

Lindsey gathered an armful of supplies and headed for the door. When she reached Ralph and Max, she nodded back toward the remaining equipment. "Could y'all help us bring all this inside?"

Ralph nodded quickly, as if eager for something to do. "Sure."

"By the way, did you get the cellar locks changed already?"

Ralph shook his head. "Jeff asked me to wait until he'd finished checking out the cellar. Didn't think it would take him this long."

Lindsey paused, calculating how long it had been since she saw Jeff. "When was this?"

"I was finishing up the back. Told him I wanted to start on the front, then do the cellar." Ralph's eyes narrowed and he glanced at his watch. His words slowed as alarm entered his voice. "Almost…an hour…"

Fear shot through Lindsey, and she shoved her supplies into Max's arms. He took them awkwardly, fighting to keep his balance. "I'm sure he's—"

"My cellar isn't that big!"

She fled into the restaurant, skidding into the kitchen. "Jeff!" She flung open the storeroom door. "Jeff!" Footsteps thundered through the restaurant as everyone followed her.

She bounded down into the cellar, stopping cold as she saw Jeff on the floor near the back door. Blood trailed from a cut on his temple, pooling under his head. His face looked pale gray in the dim light of the cellar. A sudden rush of fear chilled her to the bone.

"Call 911!" she screamed over her shoulder. "Jeff!" Lindsey dropped to her knees beside him and pressed two fingers against his jugular. "He's alive!"

She looked at the cluster of people behind her. June spoke firmly into her phone, but the others gaped at her. "Ralph, get this door open! Now! Max, go wait for the ambulance. April, get me the first aid kit from the kitchen."

Focusing again on Jeff, she held trembling fingers under his nose, where she could feel a faint movement of air. "Keep breathing. Just keep breathing."

Warm sunshine filled the cellar as Ralph opened the door to the outside.

April thumped the first aid kit down next to her. "He may be in shock."

Lindsey nodded. "There are two blankets in the storeroom. Top shelf. Wrapped in plastic. Get them."

April nodded and vanished. Her hands still fluttering with fear and adrenaline, Lindsey threw open the kit, pulling out a bottle of water. She tore open a packet of gauze and dampened it, touching it lightly to the blood on Jeff's face. Most of it was dried, and she dabbed it away until she could make out several deep gashes just above his ear. Behind her, April clattered down the steps, peeling the plastic away from the blankets. Air rushed over them as she shook them out and draped them over Jeff's body.

Lindsey knew there wasn't much more they could do, but she kept washing away the dried blood, muttering, "Wake up. Please wake up." In the distance, she could hear the siren of the ambulance.

At her side, June put a hand on her arm. "Lindsey, stop. You can't do any more. They're on the way."

Lindsey looked at her, tears stinging her eyes. "Because of me. This is because of me."

June pulled Lindsey into her arms. "He'll be all right. It'll be okay."

Lindsey leaned heavily against June. "No. It won't. Not until we stop this guy."

Jeff blinked at the man in front of him. "Nick?"

The director of the NorthCrest emergency department looked up from the computer at Jeff. "Don't even ask about going back to work. Alan told me you asked three times what happened. You're blinking at me like you can't see, and my guess is you're about to have a monster of a headache when the painkillers wear off."

"I just thought I had a drummer in my head."

"So, no, you're not going anywhere till you have another CT scan. And I have to say, I'm getting tired of sending you for these. When are y'all going to catch this guy?"

"Trying my best. Putting my head into it." Jeff winced, reaching his fingers toward the left side of his face. The effects of local anesthetic had started to subside, and the new stitches ached and pulled.

"Don't touch that."

A thousand drumsticks beat against the inside

of Jeff's skull, trying to break out. "What do you think he hit me with?"

"A meat tenderizer."

"You're joking."

"Nope. Ray told me they found one with blood on it not far from your body. The kind that looks like a mallet with points on it. Did a real number on the side of your face. Your wrist isn't broken, but it's going to hurt like crazy for a while, as well. Keep icing it and keep the wounds clean. We gave you a tetanus shot, but getting hit with something that's used on raw meat is a recipe for infection, no matter how clean Lindsey keeps it. I'm going to give you a script for some pain-killers and an antibiotic. Take them. Doctor's orders."

Jeff nodded once. His head hurt too much to nod any more than that.

Nick took off his glasses and tucked them into a pocket. "Seriously, Jeff. I'm worried about these blows to your head so close together. This time you took far too long to wake up."

"I'm fine."

"I'll be the judge of that, if you don't mind. The last one left you with a mild concussion. This one is even more serious. Last time the CT scan was a precaution. This time it's a ne-cessity." He paused and rocked forward once, then settled into a firmly planted stance. "In fact, I'm tempted to recommend that you be taken off active duty."

Jeff stiffened. "You can't—"

"Can and will. My first concern is your health, not your case. You need to heal, which could take a while. And so far, this case isn't giving you the chance. Another blow like this could mean serious brain damage, or worse. Instead of losing a case, you could lose your career. Or your life. Can't you focus on the intellectual side of the case? Let Ray work the on-the-scene stuff?"

Jeff's mouth twisted. "Lindsey...needs..." He stopped, abruptly unsure of what he wanted to say next.

Nick fell silent a few moments, watching Jeff as if his actions confirmed Nick's diagnosis. He started to speak when there was a tap on the door. Nick opened it and nodded to the person on the other side. "Your ride is here for the scan. I'll talk to Ray."

Lindsey paced the waiting area, limping.

June and April watched her, their faces knitted with concern. "Lindsey..." June began.

"No," she said, without waiting for her sister to finish. "I can't sit. He almost killed Jeff. He was inside! He knew the restaurant well enough to know he could hide in the cellar until almost everyone left. Knew it wouldn't be searched if it was still locked from the outside. If I hadn't asked Ralph to change the locks, Jeff wouldn't even have gone down there."

June stood. "The cops should have cleared it—"

Lindsey shook her head. "They didn't know there was an entrance in the storeroom. I should have said something."

"He should have had backup—"

"They were gone! He was alone! I should have—"

April stood in front of Lindsey, halting her progress. "Stop. This is *not* your fault. It's the fault of the guy who broke in and swung a meat tenderizer at a sheriff's deputy in order to escape. That guy. Not you." She took Lindsey by the shoulders and pushed her down into a chair. "Now you need to calm down and stop the pity party. This isn't about you or what you did or didn't do or could or couldn't do. I know you're a control freak, little sister, but this isn't about you or anything you can control. It's about him."

Lindsey stared at April, her cheeks heating, first with anger. *A pity party? Is that what they think?*

Well...listen to yourself.

Lindsey froze, the heat in her face becoming chagrin. "It has been about me, hasn't it?"

June and April exchanged a look of relief. April took a deep breath. "You and your restaurant. You want the case solved, but more than that, it's been about your keeping things normal and the restaurant open. Clearly that's been more important than helping them solve the problem of someone who wants to kill you. It's spreading their resources thin."

Lindsey felt ill, her stomach queasy. "I just don't want to fail. I can't let this guy make me fail!"

June sat next to her. "Have a little faith, little sister. If this is what God wants for you, you won't fail. Look at the response you got this morning. God led you here, back to us. Do you think that was a mistake? If not, then accept that He'll give you what you need to get through this."

Lindsey looked down at her hands. "You think I should shut down."

April knelt in front of her, taking both hands in hers. "RuthAnn is missing, and June and I aren't really cut out for this work."

"The customers love you."

"Because they know us. They know we're helping you out. They like that, so they'll forgive our mistakes. But not for long. You saw the chaos that happened yesterday at lunch. We ran out of food. Orders were delayed. Trying to stay open could create more problems than shutting it down."

June joined the argument. "Just close the restaurant for a few days. Give the Schneiders some needed time off, and let the Sheriff's Department narrow their focus. Give them a chance to do what they do best."

"Instead of babysitting me."

June shifted in her chair. "They'll still be doing that, but in a more secure way. It's the restaurant that's dividing their resources. Don't forget that you're the key to this. Your memory, or whatever it is that cretin thinks you remember. You can't ferret that out as long as you're worried about the Salisbury steak for table twelve."

Lindsey pulled her hands from April's and hugged herself, rocking back and forth. Her sisters made sense. Good, logical sense. But the whole thing made her gut churn. She felt tossed about, as if her dream were being tugged from her grasp in a whirlpool of unfortunate events. As if her assailant were winning by making her fail. She closed her eyes. *Lord...*

A sharp memory flashed through her mind, and Lindsey stopped moving. Her mother holding her close, rocking. *Be still, my child, and listen...* They were her mother's words, whispered as she stroked Lindsey's face with a cool cloth, following one of her father's outbursts. Lindsey let her mind drift, remembering those moments. They would wait for him to leave, then her mother would sit in a rocker and pull Lindsey into her lap, whispering, over and over *Be still, my child, and listen... Be open to hearing and the answer will come to you.*

The sound of footsteps broke through Lindsey's thoughts and her eyes opened. Ray stood in front of them, his hat in hand.

They all stood. "How is he?" Lindsey asked.

Ray hesitated, then a look of resignation crossed his face. "Not good. He hadn't really healed from the mild concussion of the first attack. This one has aggravated his condition. Nick has said if he doesn't rest, he'll recommend that Jeff be taken off active duty. Instead, I'm going to have to take him off the case—"

"What if I close the restaurant?"

Ray stopped, looking startled by the question. "What?"

Lindsey stepped closer to him. "I'll close the restaurant until this is over. Jeff and I could work on my background. It'll be mostly computer work, and we could do it in spurts, so he could rest. Whatever we turn up, y'all could do the follow-up."

"It would solve the problem of everyone being overworked," June said. "And give Jeff the chance to get the rest he needs, without being taken off the case."

Ray looked from his wife to each of the sisters in turn. "You've been plotting again."

April smiled. "We just want to help."

"Hmm." After a few moments, he nodded. "I'll talk to Jeff and Nick." He headed back to the treatment area, then paused. He looked back at the three sisters and opened his mouth to speak. Then he changed his mind, shook his head and walked away.

"What was that about?" Lindsey asked.

"He's never seen sisters in action." June grinned. "We're a formidable team when it comes to forging workable solutions."

"Workable." Lindsey sank back into a chair. The setback of closing the restaurant felt like a weight settling down on her shoulders. "It doesn't exactly feel that way to me. Feels like I'm giving up. Failing."

"Only if you let it." June stood in front of her, feet apart, hands on her hips. "In fact, a little setback might be good for you."

Lindsey stared at her sister, stunned. "What?"

April touched June on the arm, and the petite brunette relented a bit, dropping her arms to her sides. "Look, we all came from the same horror show. It worked on us to make us who we are. We're survivors. But when *we* got out, our horrors continued. When Mother died, you went into foster care—a good home, from what you've said."

Lindsey nodded, still hurt and not sure where June was headed with this.

"You had a chance to dream. To have a bit of a normal childhood. A chance to develop a long-range plan. Yeah, that plan may have come out of you going to work at fifteen, fighting for cash to help that family. But you love what you do. You planned, saved, went to school for it. In fact, since you went to work, your setbacks have been minor. You're determined, good at what you do and an amazing woman."

June took a deep breath. "But how you handle life when it doesn't go your way is as important, if not more so, as how you handle success."

A surge of anger shot through Lindsey, and she stood up. "So I should just embrace the fact this guy is ruining my business as well as trying to kill me?"

"No," said June, refusing to back down. "You should be able to see that this is a wise move in the overall scheme of trying to stop him. Success isn't always about plowing forward no matter who it hurts. Sometimes it's about taking a few steps backward so you can see the bigger picture."

Who it hurts.

Jeff. In her mind, she saw the two security guards watching over her while the rest of the Sheriff's department trickled away, already spread thin, leaving Jeff to clean up the remaining forensics tasks. Jeff should never have gone in the cellar without backup...but there was no backup.

"Also," April said softly, "the restaurant has become a weapon."

"What do you mean?"

"He's turned it against you. He's using it to hurt you, to draw you out and to hurt Jeff. It's your point of vulnerability. Shutting it down closes off one of his ways of getting to you. I know you're worried about what will happen when you reopen. But this is a small town. The people love you. They're loyal. They'll be back."

"You sound convinced."

"We are."

Behind them, Ray cleared his throat. They turned, looking at him expectantly.

"They are keeping Jeff overnight for observation. This one's pretty serious, and Nick's worried about what could happen if he gets hit again. Depending on what the CT scan shows, Nick's agreed to release him on limited duty. Desk only. No patrols. No crime scenes. In the meantime, I'm going to send a small army with you to close up the restaurant, then to your house if you need to pick up anything else. Then it's over to April and Daniel's until we get to the bottom of this. Right?"

Lindsey nodded. "Backing up in order to move ahead."

Ray paused, looking from Lindsey to his wife, then back to Lindsey. "June's been talking to you."

"How did you know?"

"Fall back and punt is my wife's favorite football play. She's the queen of second chances."

June harrumphed, then stopped, looking from Lindsey to Ray.

"What is it?" Lindsey asked.

"The book. The one in the glove compartment. We didn't get a chance to talk about it before."

Ray froze. "What about it?"

"What book?" asked April.

June turned to her older sister. "They found a book in the glove compartment of the GTO. An old, waterlogged copy of *Catcher in the Rye*."

April paled. "Oh, no."

Lindsey felt as confused as Ray looked. "What about the book?"

June moved closer to her younger sister. "You don't remember it. You went out with Daddy one day, and when y'all got home, you had a copy of *Catcher in the Rye* tucked under one arm. You picked it up wherever y'all had been. Daddy went off and beat the living daylights out of you. Called you a thief. Said you were too young to read such filth. He threw it in the toilet. You fished it out, and dried it on the windowsill. You carried that book everywhere."

Lindsey dropped down in one of the chairs. She didn't remember any of this. Didn't remember the book. Didn't remember that incident. She shook her head. "I don't..." She looked at June. "If I carried it everywhere, what happened to it?"

Lindsey barely heard April's quiet reply. "It disappeared when Mother died. You asked me about it at the funeral."

"So the book..." Ray said coldly.

June finished it. "Is a message."

Hospital rooms are never completely dark. Or quiet. Ever. Jeff decided long ago this was by design, so that no one got comfortable enough to want to stay. The longer you stayed, the more often nurses and techs made their rounds, gathering to talk outside your partially open door, occasionally dropping pens. If you stayed long enough, they graduated to dropping charts and clipboards, possibly arranging for housekeeping to overturn carts or start the floor waxer at midnight.

"Your blood pressure is still elevated." The nurse, a practical, efficient and chatty woman named Deb, had tucked, fluffed and tended to Jeff, all the while letting him know that even though she had four grandchildren she was only forty-five, and that two of those grandbabies belonged to her middle son, who was a police officer in Charlotte, so she definitely had a place in her heart for law enforcement officers.

Without appearing to even breathe, Deb continued the patter as she typed his vitals into a laptop, then scribbled the results on a whiteboard near Jeff's bed, ending with, "Any idea why it's still up?"

"Probably lack of sleep."

Deb grinned. "How's your pain level on a scale of one to ten, ten being the worst?"

"It would be a ten only if I could shoot the drummer in my head."

She nodded. "I'll check with the doc about your painkillers. Don't want to dose you too much."

Jeff returned the nod, but winced. Deb's mood turned somber, and she went silent as she peered at him a few moments. "How's your memory of the event?"

"Nada." Jeff still remembered nothing between talking to Ralph about changing the cellar locks and awakening in the ambulance. "But I don't stop in the middle of sentences anymore."

Deb smiled again, although not as broadly. "I'll take any progress. But you do need to get some rest."

"I thought y'all didn't let concussion patients sleep."

"Went out with putting butter on a burn."

"Ah, that's what the scan is for."

"Gotta love progress."

"How long before the goose egg goes down?" He pointed at the swelling around his stitches.

"Couple of days." She finished her work and paused. "Do you need anything?"

"A Wayback machine?"

"Fresh out."

"Some ice water?"

"You got it."

With that, Deb strode out of the room, pulling the door shut.

Jeff let out a long sigh and lowered the head of the bed a bit. The room reminded him of every other patient's room he'd been in, especially the empty ones his mom had someone stash him in when the babysitter hadn't shown up. Always cold and strangely unfriendly, no matter how "homelike" the designers tried to make them.

No, not just unfriendly. Remote. Alien. As if they had all been equally designed to make people feel as if they were strangers in a strange land. The nurses could make you feel welcome, as comfortable as whatever illness you had would let you be. But the rooms…you didn't really belong.

Like me in Lindsey's world.

Jeff shifted uncomfortably in the bed and adjusted the pillow. Six months. They'd known each other just over six months. For a long time he hadn't wanted to admit, even to himself, exactly how interested he was in her. He thought it revealed a lack of professionalism. After all, their friendship was based on work and their nightly runs to the bank.

But, finally, he had to admit that the protectiveness he felt ran deep, deeper than a professional relationship could account for. She'd been on his mind a lot even before that guy showed up in the GTO. Now she occupied almost every waking thought—and most of his dreams.

Should he push those feelings away and go

back to a professional relationship? He'd failed to protect her, so *could* he even go back to that? Would she trust him?

"Hey." Her voice was so soft he barely heard her.

Jeff blinked twice, not really believing he was seeing Lindsey's blond hair and blue eyes peeking through the door. "Hi."

"Can I come in?"

Jeff scrambled for the bed control and raised his head up. "Sure."

Lindsey entered and crossed the room slowly. "How are you doing?"

"All right, I guess."

"Ray said you still had some problems with your memory of the attack."

"I have no memory of it."

She winced. "That's part of the concussion?"

"So they say."

Her eyes brightened with tears. "Jeff, I'm so sorry."

"So you're the one who whacked me with a meat tenderizer?"

She hesitated, looking puzzled a second, then she straightened. The tears vanished. "Smart aleck. But you shouldn't have been in the cellar alone. If there had been backup—"

"My choice. I went alone. Just because I don't

remember doesn't mean that Ray hasn't filled in the gaps for me. And properly chewed me out in the process."

"I closed the restaurant."

Jeff froze, not quite believing what he heard. "You did? Why? Because of me? Because of this?" He couldn't believe the surge of anger he felt.

She held up her hand. "Yes, and no."

"What does that mean?"

"Yes, in part because of the attack. But mostly because of me. I've been focused on the wrong thing. The restaurant. We've been attacked. He's still threatening us. Normality *should* stop. We can go back to it later." With a sudden move forward, Lindsey grabbed one of his hands, holding it in both of hers. "And I think we've both been dancing around the edges of something we feel. That there's something between us. Whether it's love or an indelible friendship, I don't know. Right now, I don't know if I *want* to know. Right now, we just need to stop him. Does that make sense?"

Jeff looked at her, wishing suddenly that he could spend a lifetime doing just that, gazing at those eyes, her high cheekbones, those rich, full locks of hair that flowed over her shoulders. But he also recognized that they had been divided in their attention, with both the restaurant and each other. They needed to focus.

He nodded. "More sense than you may realize. But before we take this new tactic, there's something I'd like for you to do."

"What?"

"Kiss me."

Lindsey's eyes widened a bit, and she hesitated. Then, unhurriedly, she leaned toward him. He met her halfway, and their lips met with a lingering kiss that was soft and sweet. As they parted, neither spoke for a few moments, then Jeff cleared his throat. "Tomorrow, we'll be all business. Until it's done."

Lindsey licked her lips, then nodded. "Tomorrow."

Jeff stood in the cellar, but the room spun around him, a fuzzy vertigo that made it seem as if the room shifted instead of him. He turned slowly, trying to keep his balance as he examined everything around him. Shelves of equipment undulated, as if made of seawater. Light faded on and off, illuminating then darkening areas of the cellar and casting ghostly shadows all around him.

There it was, near the steps, movement that wasn't shadow. Man-shaped. The room spun faster, and as the light dimmed again, the figure moved, rushing at Jeff.

They grappled, tumbling on the floor. His strength surprised Jeff; he hadn't appeared strong. They rolled, with shades of black and white engulfing them. Too late, Jeff saw the mallet in his upraised hand.

"Ah!" Jeff jerked awake, a cry of alarm bursting from him. He looked around, head thudding with pain. The empty hospital room greeted him only with beeps, and the distant chatter of the night shift. Sweat covered his body, and Jeff thrust the covers aside, pushing down on the bed and swinging his legs over one side.

Dream. It was a dream. He recalled every moment of the dream, but even digging deep into his memory, Jeff still couldn't remember the actual events down in the cellar. But the memories were there. The dream told him they were still there.

He had to remember. Had to. Because the one thing clear in the dream threw everything Lindsey had recalled into question. She'd insisted that her attacker at RuthAnn's house had blond or red hair. The man who attacked Jeff had dark hair. He was strong, but not the extraordinary strength she'd described.

Dark hair. *Yeah, in my* dream.

He couldn't mention it yet. After all, he wasn't exactly reliable right now, mind, body…or heart.

But what if she was wrong? How would this affect the case?

Or, maybe worse, what if they were both right? There was not one attacker.

But two.

ELEVEN

The enormous full moon shining through the trees looked as if it belonged in a horror film, an old black-and-white one from the '40s, with spooky music warning of danger creeping in over the windowsill. Clouds scudded across the gleaming light, caught and tossed by the wind of a coming storm. The maple tree closest to Lindsey's window still had more than half its scarlet leaves clinging to the branches, and in the daylight looked friendly and inviting. Now, dark and backlit by the moon, the skeletal limbs clawed the air, grasping for invisible prey.

If only this was a movie.

Lindsey tensed. A sudden movement at the base of the maple sent a quick spear of fear through her. Then Polly stepped from behind the trunk, continuing on one of her rounds. Lindsey sighed and shook her head, still amazed by how well-trained and obedient the German Shepherd was. On command, the dog would circle the property, just as if she were a military officer standing guard. Lindsey felt a distinct comfort at the thought. *She's probably more reliable than most human security guards.*

Lindsey closed the heavy drapes, shutting out the scene that underscored how she felt—shadowed and filled with looming dread. Weariness filled every inch of her body, and she felt drained. The roller coaster of the past few days had taken its toll, and she wanted nothing more than to crawl under the covers and never emerge.

The events of the day lingered in her mind. After they'd left the hospital, accompanied by five of Ray's strongest, most intimidating officers, the sisters had spent several hours closing the restaurant, securing the nonperishables and giving away any food that would spoil after a few days. Lindsey tried not to think about the money she was losing, repeatedly asking God if this was the right direction.

Silence. She felt nothing, no sense of peace... but no discomfort, either. When she'd shut off the gas to the restaurant stove, Lindsey had paused, looking around at the dark wood and stainless steel of her dream. That was when she knew for certain this was the right thing to do. Closing the restaurant would allow them to focus on the case. Still, even knowing it was the right thing to do, Lindsey couldn't shake the feeling of finality, as if she were bidding the building some sort of final farewell.

Their next stop, the little house she rented from Max, hadn't required as much time or emotion. Once more Lindsey mentally went through the rooms, taking inventory to see if she'd forgotten anything she needed or wanted. Nothing came to mind then or now as she eased into bed, plumping the pillows in the high four-poster bed and snuggling in for her nightly routine.

She looked around the room, again grateful to April and Daniel for opening their home to her. This bed, the entire room, was more elegant and expensive than any Lindsey had ever slept in. While she knew it had passed to her sister from Aunt Suke, Lindsey couldn't help thinking how far they had all come from the days when they lived in fear of their father, watching their mother make filling meals from the meager cash he would sometimes bring home.

They'd had their trials, but God, in His time, had been good to all of them.

Lindsey reached for her grandmother's Bible. She handled it carefully, making sure none of the plethora of items stuck between the pages slipped free. The Bible bulged with an assortment of photos, letters, quotations, sermon excerpts, notes on Bible lessons, postcards, even a slip of fabric that someone had told her was a man's collar, from back in the days when shirt collars were sold separately. Just as the diary was a glimpse into her mother's life, the Bible opened Lindsey's grandmother to her. At one time, in her teens, Lindsey had gone through the Bible, examining each article, but she hadn't looked at most of them in years. To her they were as much a part of the Bible as the thin pages and silk ribbon markers.

She knew which passage she needed tonight—the same one she'd relied on so often in the past, Psalm 91. As she read, however, one verse stood out: "Thou shalt not be afraid for the terror by night; nor for the arrow that flieth by day."

Lindsey put her hand flat on the page and closed her eyes. "Lord, I know You will take care of us. You always have. I thought it was hard to trust You with my dreams. I never realized how much harder it is to trust You with my fears. Please forgive my doubts and strengthen my faith."

Lindsey sat still for a while, just trying to open her mind and heart to God, to listen. Still…nothing. No insight. No sense of peace. But no disquiet, either. Just…evenness.

The clock at the base of the stairs chimed

11:15 p.m. Polly, now back inside, moved through the house, her nails clicking rhythmically on the wooden floors. Soft male and female voices echoed down the hall, perhaps April and Daniel…or a television. Aunt Suke laughed, perhaps at something she read. In the distance, a faint rumbling of thunder, foretelling the arrival of one of the autumn storms that regularly shook the central Tennessee area. Outside the wind picked up, the leaves rustling with a quiet fury.

The sounds of a normal life.

Lindsey's eyes opened wide as her chest tightened with a sudden desire for this to continue. Normalcy. A home, family around her, a place of safety and love. It had never been part of her life, never been part of her dreams. She'd never thought it possible.

"Is this what You want for me?" she whispered. "What You wanted me to see?"

The craving did not ease, and Lindsey finally nodded. She closed the Bible and reached to return it to the bedside table. As she did, an envelope slid from within its pages and landed on the floor softly. Lindsey frowned, got out of bed and retrieved it. She recognized it immediately, a letter her mother had written to her grandmother not long before she died, although she didn't remember much about the contents other than the nature of it that was so unlike the short, sensible daily entries of the woman who wrote the diary. Lindsey had found it hard to read, and only had done so once. Now, some of the words stood out, and a deep cold settled over her, chilling her to the bone, and tears slid down her cheeks.

Dearest Mama,
Things are worse than usual here, and you are right. My mind is not what it was. I still can't seem to remember much, even after all these months, keeping straight the details that I need to raise my girls. I feel like a complete simpleton most days. Perhaps he is right about that.

He is not the same as he was before the incident, either. I'd like to think he's sorry he hurt me so bad that time, but that's just foolish. He's never cared about that, though he's not hit me as much since someone whacked him around. Still withdrawn, and more silent. If I didn't know better, I'd say he was afraid of something. Maybe whoever beat him up?

I don't know, but he's been even worse since they found that woman's body. Bones, really. She's been missing more than a year.

He throws something at the TV and storms out every time it's on the news.

You probably saw it on the news. Karen something. She's from the neighborhood, a few streets over. Shame. I hear she was a sweet girl. They're still looking for her killer.

I'm writing to ask if you'll take July, if something happens to me. He's threatened to throw them all out on the streets. I know June and April will be all right. They're gone most of the time already, staying away from him. But July, she won't have a place. So young, I don't want her on the streets. Let me know.

Love,

Evie

Lindsey leaned heavily against the bed, then slid to the floor, hugging herself and drawing her knees up. Heavy sobs broke through as the words bounced around in her mind.

Karen something. From the neighborhood. A sweet girl.

"*Who beat up your father?*"

"*Karen's husband.*"

They're still looking for her killer.

"Dear Lord, help me. What in the world did I see? What happened to Karen?"

Inhaling deep, gulping breaths, Lindsey forced herself to her feet. "I have to see Jeff." She twisted around, confused. "No, not see. Call." She spun around again, looking for her cell phone.

Thunder boomed, and Lindsey jumped, crying out, turning toward the window. Lightning flashed around the edges of the drapes, like a camera flash in another room. Lindsey started again, her heart racing. Then the rain began, splashing hard against the window.

Shaking, Lindsey went to the window and pushed back the drapes again. Darkness reigned now, the moon sequestered behind the rolling thunderheads. A lone dusk-to-dawn light in the yard did what it could to pierce through the murky rain, and floodlights under the eaves spotlighted round areas of glistening grass.

It was raining that day, too.

Lindsey gasped, her hand covering her mouth. She didn't know where that thought came from, but she knew all too well what day her memory spoke of.

The day her mother found her cowering in the garage. She'd been wet. Soaked.

"I need to talk to Jeff." She turned away from

the window, crossed the room and snatched her cell phone up off the bedside table. Then she stopped, staring at it. *No. He's in the hospital. Medicated.*

Lindsey looked around the room as if searching for something. "I need to…" She wanted desperately to act on this information. No way she could sleep. "I need to get on the internet."

Her computer remained packed deep in one of her boxes, but she didn't have access in the bedroom anyway. Grabbing her robe and sliding her feet into her slippers, she opened the door and headed downstairs. Daniel and April kept a home office in a butler's pantry off the kitchen. As security conscious as Daniel was, it was probably password-protected, but she had to try. At least she could find some paper and do some brainstorming.

Finding her way using the night-lights, she padded downstairs, down the wide hallway from the foyer to the kitchen, and into their office. Snapping on a desk lamp, she sat down and booted up the computer. Sure enough, it asked for a password.

Could she guess? She didn't have June's savvy way with computers, but desperation was the mother of all kinds of invention. She thought about her sister, then typed in *jamandjellies*.

Beep. No access.

Lindsey scowled in frustration. Surely it was more than a random series of letters. Most people picked a password they could remember, something close to them.

pollysuke. Beep. No access.

"Try Evelyn May."

Lindsey yelped and spun around in the chair. Aunt Suke stood behind her, a mischievous grin on her face. Polly pressed against Suke's leg, looking somber.

"I'm sorry. I didn't mean to wake anyone up."

Aunt Suke's long gray hair trembled as she chuckled. "You didn't. Old people don't sleep like you young folks. I'm up several times a night. Sometimes I go right back to sleep. Other nights it takes some warm milk or cocoa to send me back to bed. With all this thunder booming overhead, I knew it would be a cocoa night. Maybe a late-night movie." She nodded at the computer. "Try it."

Lindsey hesitated. "That's my mother's name."

"And your niece's. In a few months."

Lindsey stared at the older woman as the words sunk in. Hard. Her mouth gaped. "April's *pregnant?*"

Aunt Suke put her finger to her lips. "Shh.

They haven't told anyone. Don't want anyone to know yet. So you don't know it, either."

Guilt clenched Lindsey as she thought about the mornings April hadn't felt well. The oversize T-shirts. Other signs. They were all there, but in her determination to keep the Coffee-Time Café going, Lindsey had not noticed them. "She should have told me. She's worked so hard for me."

"Hush, girl. She's your sister. None of it put the baby in danger. She wouldn't have done that. But we all willingly sacrifice for the ones we love."

The words sank in. Had she ever willingly sacrificed for someone she loved? Ever?

No.

Aunt Suke pointed at the computer again. "Try it. Daniel changes the password the first of every month, but I think that's this month's."

Lindsey turned back and typed in *evelynmay*. A pause, then the computer completed its start-up cycle. She almost cheered, and turned to find Aunt Suke dragging another chair into the office. She pulled it up to the desk and sat down.

"Excellent. It worked. So let's see what you needed so badly you couldn't sleep." She peered expectantly at the computer, then at Lindsey, who knew the surprise showed on her face. "It's a night of shared secrets, my dear."

She was right, and Lindsey recognized it. Even though they barely knew each other, Aunt Suke treated her as if she were family. And maybe they were.

Lindsey opened a web browser. "I need to find out if it was raining the day Karen disappeared."

"Well, you could have just asked me that."

Lindsey turned to face Aunt Suke again. "You know what I'm talking about?"

"Sure. Karen Lawson. It was big news around here for a few months. They showed her picture on the news every other night."

"How come no one I asked had ever heard of her?"

"Well, honey, that was, what, fifteen, twenty years ago? Y'all were all just kids. It wasn't like a shuttle explosion or something national that everyone would know about. And scores of women have disappeared over the years. They stay on the news a few weeks, then they're replaced by the next one. But if you want to know local news from twenty years ago, you ask old people like me."

"So what happened?"

Aunt Suke frowned a few moments. "Now you'll want to confirm with what you find on the net, but near as I remember it, Karen Lawson picked her kids up from school every day and dropped them at her mother's. She worked second shift as a nurse. Her husband was some big-shot attorney who was never home.

"One day, Karen doesn't show. Grandma gets worried and calls the police. The kids were at different schools, and the police find out she picked up the youngest but not the high schoolers. Sometime between the two pickups, she and the little girl vanished. They found her van at the airport, thought she was probably a runaway wife. Husband took the two older kids and disappeared into Mexico. About nine months later, a jogger found Karen's bones." Aunt Suke's mouth twisted. "Her daughter's, too."

"Did they suspect her husband?"

Aunt Suke shrugged. "No idea. If I remember, they couldn't prove anything. No witnesses. No evidence. Nothing."

"But it was raining the day she vanished?"

"Buckets. I remember because there's this memorable shot of the police department spokesman trying to talk to the reporters. He had a floppy hat on, and it was pouring so hard, it kept folding the brim down in his eyes. Stuck out because it was a funny image in the midst of a serious subject. Behind him some of the police were coming in and out of the house, all bundled up against the rain. The husband complained later that all they'd done that day was ruin his carpeting. He sued them for the damages."

"You're kidding."

"Nope. Lots of stupidity going on about that one." Aunt Suke took a deep breath and absently stroked Polly's head. "Anyway, you'll want to confirm it, but that gives you something to go on." She paused. "Why did you want to know if it was raining that day?"

Lindsey licked her lips. "Because, Aunt Suke, I think buried somewhere deep in this thick head of mine are memories of that day. I think I saw what happened to Karen Lawson."

TWELVE

"You have to walk around, Mr. Gage."

This morning's nurse, all five-feet nothing of her, was a no-nonsense Hispanic woman who made Jeff think she could run the hospital all by her lonesome, thank you very much. Her orders had been firm but gentle, even if Jeff knew exactly what she meant. *Stop being lazy and get yourself up out of that bed.*

"Shoes. I need shoes."

With clipped movements, she pulled his shoes from the closet and set them on the floor beside the bed. "You show no other signs of brain injury. Your vitals are good. So if you can walk unassisted, the doctor said he would discharge you. I have to watch you."

Jeff stuffed his feet into his shoes without untying them and stood up, feeling like an idiot in his hospital gown and street shoes. "How far do I have to go?"

She checked the saline bag that had dripped

fluids and painkillers into his system overnight, then unsnapped his IV tube. "To the door and back. That should be enough to judge your balance."

Jeff did the task, sat down on the bed, then looked up at her. "Okay?"

"I'll call it in. Once approval is received, I'll send someone to remove the IV from your arm. Sit tight."

Like there was anything else he could do. He kicked off the shoes and sat in one of the chairs for a moment. He was astonished that he still felt a bit disoriented, as if the world was not in complete sync with his head.

Memory of the attack still had not returned, although he'd had several violent dreams in which he faced a vicious confrontation. Unlike the first dream, there had been no spinning rooms, and he hadn't felt fear or panic in the dreamed fights. In fact, he'd been so calm that he'd almost felt numb. Peaceful, as if he knew the outcome. He'd dreamed of Lindsey only once, a faraway figure caught in a storm.

Jeff stood up. He needed a plan for the day, especially if he was going to be deskbound. Solving most cases usually involved a lot of pure detective work anyway, lots of phone calls, online searches and interviews. But he needed a methodical plan.

He pulled his clothes from the closet and dressed, taking care not to catch his shirt on the IV still taped securely inside his elbow. Then he found a notepad and a pen in a drawer. First on the agenda would be to get those replacement part numbers from Troy, who had readily agreed to help him with the vendors, if it came to that. Those he could research online, find probable vendors. If he or Troy could get shipping addresses from them, he might come closer to finding the owner of that car.

A tap on the door, followed by a gruff, "Gage, you up?" announced Ray Taylor's arrival. When Jeff told him the plan for the day, Ray nodded. "That could take most of the day. When did you plan to interview Lindsey again?"

Jeff hesitated. "I hadn't planned to."

Ray's eyebrows arched in question.

"I thought it might be better if you did the second interview."

The eyebrows didn't move.

"I thought you might be more...objective. I've clearly made some errors on this case that may be emotionally based."

Ray just waited.

Jeff cleared his throat. "Some of the mistakes

I've made seem to be because I've focused more on Lindsey than on the events and facts of the case. She and I even talked about it yesterday. We agreed that we both needed to focus more on the case, so it would probably be better for her if you took over any further interviews with her."

"Better for her."

Jeff straightened. "And for the case. Better for the case, of course."

"Hmm."

"I can stick with the forensics. The research—that's what I'm best at."

Ray's cell phone buzzed on his hip. He pulled it out and glanced at it. "That's the fourth one today so far." He replaced it. "You probably have just as many."

"What? Messages?"

Ray nodded. "From Lindsey. Apparently your cell phone is off. A fact she informed me of about five o'clock in the morning. And every hour since."

"Is something wrong?"

"Probably not, or Daniel would have notified me. Her last message mentioned that she'd found out some things about Karen."

"What?"

"Guess I'll find out when I interview her."

Jeff's eyes narrowed. "Cruel, boss."

Ray barely cracked a smile. "Your call. You about ready to get out of here?"

"Waiting for a nurse to remove the IV."

"I'll go see if I can speed up the process any. In the meantime, think about the last time you ran away from something you needed to learn. How'd that turn out?"

Ray strode out, leaving Jeff annoyed and more than a bit confused. *What kind of question was that? I wish he wouldn't do that.*

But the challenge was on the table. What else had he run away from? Jeff racked his brain, going over times in the past when they'd come up against something in a case for which no one on the team had the know-how. Jeff, by nature a puzzle solver, was the one who usually dug in and found what was needed or learned some new skill. It's why he had wound up the sole forensic tech in the sheriff's department.

Thanks for trying to make me feel even worse, boss. You know I don't ever *run from...*

Oh. Lindsey.

"I really hate it when you do that," Jeff muttered to the empty room.

Twenty minutes later, they left the hospital and headed for the station, where Lindsey waited, printouts in hand.

* * *

"His name is Todd Lawson. Karen's husband."
Lindsey stood at one end of the conference-room
table and handed duplicate printouts to Ray and
Jeff. "Aunt Suke remembered the case, so it gave
me a place to start." She pointed to the copy of
Catcher in the Rye, which lay on the table between the two men. "That confirms that June
was correct about the book being a message.
The name of Karen Lawson's teenage son inside
the front cover connects it to the Lawson family
and the GTO. If that is, in fact, the book I carried
around, it probably means that my father had an
affair with Karen Lawson." She paused, swal-
lowing hard. "One of my father's strangest cruel-
ties was to take me along when he was sleeping
around, just to torment my mother.

"See, it's all starting to make a weird kind of
sense." Lindsey tried to keep the excitement out
of her voice, without much success, as she sum-
marized what she and Aunt Suke had found in
the wee hours of the morning. "Todd Lawson has
been missing since the mid-1990s. Disappeared
sometime after his wife and daughter did. When
those bones turned up and it was determined
they belonged to Karen and Sasha Lawson, the
police reopened her case as a possible homicide,
even though there wasn't enough evidence with

the remains to indicate murder. He and his two sons had already moved to Mexico. He claimed it was to escape the publicity about Karen's disappearance. The police went down to interview him, but he and the boys were gone, along with a truck and most of their cash."

"Never found?" Jeff asked.

Lindsey shook her head. "The Nashville police still consider it an open case, but a cold one. They don't expect to solve it unless new evidence turns up. If you read between the lines, most people think Todd did it."

Jeff kept taking notes, not looking up even as he asked questions. "Did you talk to anyone on the force?"

Lindsey hesitated. "No. This was all from reports I found online. I thought y'all would have to contact the NPD."

"We do." Ray's clipped words matched his unmoving, military posture.

Lindsey looked from one man to the other, her confidence wavering for the first time. Jeff refused to look at her. Ray never took his eyes off her, but he might as well have been watching a post for all the emotion he revealed. Didn't they want this info? She took a deep breath and handed each of them another printout of a picture that took up most of the page.

"This is Todd Lawson's last DMV photo."

Ray looked at the photo briefly, then added it to his stack. Jeff pulled it closer but barely glanced at it.

Lindsey's confusion gave way to frustration, and she tapped the table. "Guys, I know it's old, but if you look closely, you'll see it looks a lot like the sketch I did. Same bone structure, same creepy blue eyes."

Jeff picked up the photo, focused on it, then his eyes widened and he sat very still, staring.

"What is it?" Ray asked him.

Jeff muttered something Lindsey couldn't understand, then stood and went to the other end of the table. "Close your eyes."

"What?"

"Humor me. Close your eyes a minute."

Lindsey crossed her arms.

"Please."

Finally, she relented and closed her eyes. When he spoke, Jeff's voice was even, almost comforting, hypnotic.

"Clear your mind. You've been focused on this all night. You're tired. Think about something else. Aunt Suke. Polly. June at her wedding. Remember? She was beautiful. You were meeting a lot of people from here for the first time. Moving around. Everyone was new to you. Think about all those faces, looking among them for the ones familiar to you. June. April. Ray. Daniel."

Jeff's words had the desired effect. Lindsey's mind drifted back to June's wedding. It had been a beautiful day, but her hands had been ice cold, she was so nervous. So many new people. The sisters she hadn't seen in far too many years. Lindsey found her mind wandering among them, the ones she'd known then, the ones she'd gotten to know since.

He fell silent for a few minutes. "Now open your eyes and tell me what you see."

Lindsey opened her eyes. At the end of the table stood the young man who'd tried to kidnap her. She gasped and stepped backward, fumbling for a chair, falling heavily into it.

Jeff moved the picture from in front of his face. "You see it, don't you?"

Lindsey fought to catch her breath. "Don't do that!"

Ray stood, concern etching his face for the first time. "What's wrong?"

Jeff turned the picture toward his boss, tapping it excitedly. "The guy who attacked Lindsey that first night. The one in the hospital in a coma. He has to be Todd Lawson's son. Has to be."

Lindsey felt numb. "Why didn't I see it?"

Jeff sat down next to her. "Because we haven't

been focusing on the guy in the coma. After all, he was a blank slate. No evidence. No prints in the system. Nothing to look at. We've had our minds on the second guy, who was clearly the larger threat. When you looked at this picture, you naturally tried to see in it the outline of the guy you sketched. And you're right, it's there. But Todd at this age looks a lot more like the kid in the hospital than the man in the mask."

Lindsey looked at him, recovering her excitement. "Now what do we do?"

Jeff rubbed his hands together. "First, I'll call NPD, see if they have anything on the Lawsons that could be tested. Karen and Sasha disappeared before DNA was in wide usage, but NPD has a good rep for the quality of their preserved evidence. They recently solved a murder from the '70s with DNA extracted from carefully preserved evidence from the scene. I'll ask the lab to run a familial match on the kid in the coma. They'll also have the most recent whereabouts on Todd Lawson."

Lindsey frowned and pointed at the printouts. "These say that he disappeared into Mexico and hasn't been seen since."

"Yes, but reporters get tired and move on. Cold case detectives are like snapping turtles. They never let go. Just because it didn't make the papers doesn't mean they haven't known where he's been."

"So now we just need to find Todd Lawson." Jeff nodded. "Before he finds you."

They made the call to Nashville from the speakerphone in the conference room, agreeing that Jeff would do the questioning. Once it started, Detective Mark Bradley let them know right away that they'd hit a sweet spot. He hungered to solve the Lawson murders. Jeff took lots of notes and tried to maintain a professional demeanor. And he could tell the NPD detective, a twenty-five-year veteran of the force, did, as well. But it was hard to fight the idea that this might be the lightning strike that solved one of the highest-profile unsolved murders in Nashville's history. Harder still with Lindsey hovering over him, leaning against his shoulder as they listened to the detective on the speakerphone.

"Absolutely right. We never stopped tracking the guy." Detective Bradley took a deep drag on a cigarette and blew out the smoke slowly. The sound was so distinct, Jeff thought he could smell smoke. In the background, Bradley's car engine idled smoothly. "Todd Lawson is scum, lower than a snake's belly, even when he was a practicing attorney. Sleaziest of the sleaze. The neighborhood where they lived was known for its domestic abuse calls, and there was more than one visit from the local guys to that address."

"Any other possibilities for Karen and Sasha's deaths?" Jeff asked.

"None." Mark's voice was firm, but then he paused. "There's evidence we never released to the press."

"Anything that you could pull DNA evidence from?" Jeff asked.

Bradley hesitated. "Possibly. You have something to compare it with?"

"Our suspect. The lab already has his DNA." Jeff paused and cleared his throat. "We think he may be Lawson's son."

Bradley muttered a curse under his breath. "We've got fairly recent shots of the boys from their place down in Mexico. I'll pull those, as well. This could be huge. Our current evidence is close but no cigar. Not enough to convict Lawson but enough to rule out the only other suspect we were looking at. Not enough for Mexico to extradite but enough for a judge to give me a standing warrant for his financial records. I pull 'em whenever I have time, at least monthly, just to make sure he's stayed on the southern side of the border."

"Recent activity?"

"Nope, but it's been hinky for a while, so we've been watching a little more closely. For the past four months, he's been pulling larger amounts of cash from his bank accounts, taking out advances on the credit cards. We thought he might be up to something, but had no clues as to what it might be. Then all credit cards, phone records, everything, went silent about three weeks ago. That's when we figured he's back in the country."

"He's done this before?"

"About once every other year or so. Two years ago we think he met his parents in Laredo for money and some family time. By the time we discovered it, he was back in Mexico. He's careful, and he does it so seldom that I've only recently spotted a pattern in his purchases right before he goes off the grid."

"He doesn't get caught at the border?"

"We think he has friends, partners in the illegal-alien underground. A guaranteed way into the country without getting caught, but dangerous. Those thugs sometimes shoot people just for the fun of it. I know a woman who's here legally, but her brother tried to come over illegally. One of the cartels stopped the bus in the middle of the desert, demanded two grand from everyone on board. Right then. This is after they'd already paid a small fortune for a seat on the bus. If you couldn't wire it by cell phone or give over the cash, they shot you, left your body for the buzzards. Rough stuff."

"I'll say. Any sign Lawson has ever been beyond Texas?"

"A few years ago, there was a sighting in Wichita. Couldn't confirm it."

Lindsey stiffened. "Wichita?"

Jeff nodded, remembering the exchanges with June about the GTO car parts. "Any idea what he was doing in Kansas?"

"None. We can't even confirm he was there."

"So you have no idea if his trip would have anything to do with car parts."

Mark Bradley fell silent so long, Jeff thought he'd lost the connection. "Mark?"

"You have to tell me why you asked that." Bradley's voice had changed, dropping into a gruff bass level.

Jeff and Lindsey looked at each other, and Jeff took a deep breath. "There's a classic GTO involved in the crime. A 1968 model. We're thinking some of the replacement parts might have come from the Wichita area. We haven't traced them yet, but that's the direction we're headed."

"Title?"

"Scrubbed."

Bradley let out a long whistle. "I'll be a—" He broke off. "If I ever get my hands on that…"

"What is it?" Jeff asked.

"Back when he was practicing, Lawson's main business was getting car thieves off. We figured he also had a side business of cleaning titles, but that's not easy to prove. For a while, though, we had a lot of cars with salvage titles vanish off the face of the planet. They were supposed to be destroyed, but they had a habit of disappearing from the salvage yard. We baited a few, were able to prove they didn't go into the crusher, but never could track them after that. There's a huge market for American cars in Mexico. That's how he's making money down there. That slimeball is still at it. You know the topper? Our eyes on his place tell us he has a fleet of classic cars in a barn. Restores them as a hobby, then auctions them off."

"He's got to get those parts somewhere."

The excitement in Bradley's voice escalated. "You track those parts, Gage. You get us a connection between those parts and Lawson. With that, we'll have enough to bring him back to stand trial for theft. You'll have enough to charge him with kidnapping. That'll give you a chance to tie him to the murders."

"We'll do the best we can. Get me that DNA, would you?"

"You got it. Keep me posted."

Jeff pressed the button to end the connection. Lindsey leaped from her chair with a squeal and threw her arms around Jeff. Jeff's eyes widened as he awkwardly returned the hug, but she didn't seem to notice.

She broke away and gave a little happy dance. "Thank You, God! Thank you, Nashville! And thank you, June!"

Ray nodded in agreement. "It does take a village sometimes."

Jeff shrugged. "Now we just have to catch him. And have enough evidence that something sticks." He looked at Lindsey. "And we still don't know why he's targeted you. Why he wants you dead badly enough to put his life at risk."

Lindsey's mood changed suddenly, from giddy to morose. She sank into one of the chairs. "He thinks I saw something that day. The day Karen disappeared…the day she died. I remember during the attack at RuthAnn's house, he called me a snoopy kid. Said I always had been."

Ray's brows furrowed. "So why wait all this time to come after you? Where's he been?"

She opened her mouth to speak, then fell silent, her gut twisting painfully as she realized where this was headed—somewhere she didn't want to go. Someplace she hadn't been in over fifteen years.

"Lindsey?" Jeff prodded. "Let the memories come."

She shook her head.

"Lindsey?"

Every muscle in her back tensed, an automatic reaction to memories she wanted left buried. Maybe…maybe she could stop before it went all the way....

She blurted the first words, "It's not where *he's* been. It's where *I've* been." She took a deep breath and started again, focusing on the fingers that twitched in her lap. "It all happened during the same period. Karen vanished the same day my dad got beat almost to death and my mother found me, wet and beaten, in the garage. The dates in her diary match what I found online. Shortly after that, my dad killed my mom. My name changed legally to Lindsey Presley, but while I was in school, I called myself Lindsey Purvis—the name of my foster family. I wanted nothing to do with the Presleys. I didn't use that name again until I went to culinary school, then moved down here."

Jeff let out a sigh of recognition. "So he didn't know where you were, even if you were still alive."

Ray snorted. "Bet that was a shock to his system. Wonder how he found out."

Lindsey continued staring at her lap. She *so* did not want to go any farther. "No idea."

But Jeff straightened suddenly. "Yes, you do. Remember? What he said to you at the wreck. 'You should be dead. Again.' He's tried to kill you before. He tried to kill you that day."

The pain in Lindsey's stomach began to radiate outward. She couldn't look at them. "I think so. But I still don't remember."

Ray put the pieces together, as well. "He tried to kill you. And he was the one who beat up your father." He looked at Jeff. "Too bad we can't talk to Presley."

Lindsey winced, and silence filled the room. Pain laced through every muscle as Lindsey warred with herself. What she needed to say would be a betrayal of her sisters, but perhaps it was time to stop ignoring the truth.

Ray cleared his throat and stood up. "I'm off to other things. Jeff, let me know what you find out about those car parts."

When Jeff didn't respond, Lindsey glanced up to find him watching her intently. His next words were softer, gentler than she had ever heard.

"Whatever it is, it'll be all right. We're here for you. We won't leave you."

Ray had stopped at the door. Now they both watched her, waiting silently.

She took a deep breath. "You could ask my father."

THIRTEEN

Ray and Jeff exchanged confused glances. "I thought your father was dead," Jeff whispered.

Ray returned to sit at the table. "April and June both talk as if he had passed away."

Lindsey let out a long breath. "They want him to be. To them, he is. They even refer to him as if he were dead. They certainly never plan to see him again."

"Where is he?"

Lindsey barely got the word out. "Riverbend."

Ray finished it. "Maximum Security."

She gave a quick nod. "He got life without parole for killing my mother. Repeat offender status, for previous arrests. I mentioned it once after I got down here, and my sisters both acted like I'd tried to lure a beast from his lair. I didn't want to say anything, but if you found out..."

Jeff placed a gentle hand on her arm. "Do you think he'd help us?"

She shrugged. "Doubt it. He hated us. Hated

being a father. But I also doubt he has any love for Todd Lawson. If he thought he could get revenge…maybe."

"Worth a try," Ray said.

"It'll take a few days to arrange, however." He hesitated. "Do you want to go?"

Lindsey felt the color drop from her face and the room start spinning. She gripped the table. "I don't think…I don't think I could handle it."

Ray stood. "I'll call the warden and see what we need to do. Y'all get on to the car parts angle."

Lindsey smiled. "Y'all? Me, too?"

Ray looked as if she'd stated the obvious. "Of course. I'm tired of spreading my people out all over the county. *He* has to be here or at home, and I want *you* here or at Daniel's. If you're going to be here, you might as well be useful. It's not like I want you hanging out watching television all day." With that, Ray closed the door behind him.

"They are so suited for each other."

Jeff looked up at her, puzzlement clouding his face. "Who?"

She gestured toward the door. "Ray and June." She shrugged. "It's just a thought that's been in the back of my mind the past couple of days. I haven't been around him much since I moved here. I was so focused on getting my business up and running. I didn't mean to ignore people or shut anyone out, but it just felt like..." She reached out and closed her fist in midair, as if trying to catch something. "The dream was that close. Just out of reach. And if I lost focus even for a second, it would just..." She spread her fingers. "Poof. Be gone." Her voice dropped to a whisper and she flattened her hand on the table, fingers spread. "Everything would be gone. One more time. I'm so tired of starting over."

Lindsey realized that Jeff was staring intently at her, and she felt her cheeks heat up. "Sorry. I guess that sounds selfish."

He shook his head. "Not at all. It's a wondrous thing to be able to pursue a dream. Not everyone gets the chance. We both have."

"That's right. You wanted to work with the LAPD."

"They trained me. Best in the world. I wouldn't trade it for anything. Although I'm not exactly living up to the training right now." Lindsey started to protest, but Jeff held up a finger to stop her. "What we both need to realize is that sometimes your dreams come true...and sometimes what comes true is the real dream."

"Mother used to whisper to me, 'Never underestimate God's plan for your life.' When we were cowering from my father, I thought that was a joke."

"And now?"

"I think she could see a bigger picture. I don't know what that was. Don't know if I ever will. But I know she believed in something I couldn't even dream of."

"I want you to meet my mother—" Jeff stopped abruptly and Lindsey was surprised to see his face flush. "I don't mean, like, you know, time to meet the parents—" He stopped again.

Lindsey waited, eyebrows arched, trying hard not to grin. "I'm sure she's very sweet."

Jeff blew out a long breath. "You can be a little cruel."

She laughed. "I just wanted to see where you were going with it."

He circled his hand in the air. "Dreams. Big picture. My mom has been the queen of the big picture after my dad died, even after her cancer. I think y'all would…" He took a deep breath. "Want to call Troy?"

"I think we'd better," Lindsey said quickly, grateful for the change of subject.

Jeff dialed the number, and Troy answered with "Well, it's about time."

Jeff grinned. "It hasn't been that long."

"Eons!" Troy pronounced, falling into his favorite redneck persona. "Rust is eatin' away at the underbelly, and kudzu has done busted down the doors and took over the engine block. A few more days, you wouldn't even see it anymore. Maybe a little an-tennie sticking up amongst the greenery."

"Sorry we kept you waiting."

"You on the speakerphone?"

"We are."

"We? That pretty little Yankee there with you?"

"Hi, Troy. You know I'm from Nashville."

"Yeah, but you done spent more'n six months in Chicago. It'll take a bit for you to get your South'run back on. Maybe you should indulge in a little poke sallet—"

"Part numbers?" interrupted Jeff.

"You got a pen?"

"Ready and waiting."

In a clear, businesslike voice, Troy read off a series of parts and serial numbers, which he then made Jeff read back to him. "Need to make sure they're right," he explained. "One number off and you'd think they came from Waikiki instead of Wichita."

"We'll be careful."

"Good. Oh, and Miss Lindsey?"

"Yes, Troy?"

"Don't you worry none. We're going to get

you through this safe and sound. Gage there is as good as they come."

Lindsey looked at Jeff and grinned. "I know."

"Goodbye, Troy," Jeff said insistently, breaking the connection. He looked at the paper. "Quite a list. That GTO must have been in bad shape."

"Why don't we split it?"

"Deal. C'mon, I'll show you where we do this." He led her into the bullpen area of the station and offered her the desk of an officer out on patrol. "Kenny won't be back for a few hours, and I know he locks everything up before he leaves. Good practice." He logged her into the computer and showed her the sites that they used to search for car parts. "Everything is centralized now, and legitimate vendors report part sales so they can be tracked."

"So, if I buy an alternator at Pep Boys in Nashville…"

"…a cop in Dallas could look up the serial number and find out that you'd spent your money in Nashville."

"Sounds like that would be a help with car theft."

"Exactly the point."

Lindsey looked up at him. "Is this going to get you guys in trouble, my helping the police?"

Jeff shook his head. "Not with this. You're just gathering public information the same way you did last night with Aunt Suke. I'll make the calls to the vendors because I can't let you represent yourself as an agent of the police."

Lindsey nodded and set to work. The first four serial numbers on her list turned up as nonexistent. In three cases, there weren't enough numbers for the part. With the fourth, there were too many. Still, within an hour, they had a list of five vendors, all in the Wichita area, who had sold parts that were now on the 1968 GTO.

"It's a start," Jeff said. "If you'll verify the phone numbers, I'll start call—"

Ray flung open his office door and pointed at Jeff, then Lindsey. "Let's go. And grab your forensics kit."

They didn't hesitate. "What's going on?" Lindsey asked.

"We're going to the hospital. They found RuthAnn."

They both got into Ray's cruiser, barely buckling up before he roared out of the parking space, blue lights flashing. Lindsey grabbed the door handle as he swung the heavy car expertly through the small-town streets until he picked up the main highway into Springfield. Then she felt the real power of the car as he increased speed.

"Where did they find her?" Jeff asked.

"The Skyliner."

Jeff made a derisive noise.

"What's that?"

Jeff twisted in the front seat to look back at her. "A motel. They rent the rooms in three-hour segments and seldom change the sheets."

Lindsey understood. "Why was she in a place like that?"

"A lot of turnover means no one pays any attention to anyone else," Ray said. "We don't know if she's been there since she was taken or more recently, and apparently, neither does the management. 'Walter Mitty' signed the register two weeks ago and paid for the room a month in advance."

"Why did they check the room?" Jeff asked.

"Seems the Do Not Disturb sign blew off the doorknob and the maid thought she could clean. Found RuthAnn instead." He glanced briefly at Lindsey in the rearview. "She was tied to the bed and gagged with duct tape. She's been worked over pretty hard. Nick said they're running the regular battery of tests, but he warned me that she's pretty hysterical."

"What did that monster do to her?"

He hesitated, then replied, "No idea. She's asked for a lawyer."

Lindsey's emotions cycled from horror to confusion. "Why would she need a lawyer?"

"That's what I'm hoping she'll tell you when she comes back to her senses. Jeff, I'll collect any of the physical evidence Nick and his team may have salvaged. Then I'll take the kit and go to the crime scene, see what else might turn up. You stay with Lindsey and RuthAnn."

Lindsey huddled in the backseat, pressing into the corner, her mind swirling with possible explanations. She knew all too well the kind of experiences that could make you want to keep quiet and never mention a word about it ever again. But a lawyer? Lawyers, good ones, protected their clients. *But why would RuthAnn need protection from us?* Only one answer kept coming to mind, and Lindsey shuddered at the thought.

RuthAnn was somehow involved in all this.

Lindsey shook her head. No, there had to be something else. *Suspend judgment. We need to talk to her.*

When they entered the E.R., one of the nurses spotted them and waved them over, then escorted them to Nick's office, a room as distant in mood from the bustling roar of the emergency room as a monastery from a nightclub. Thick carpet, plants and dark wood cast a soothing ambiance over the room. Nick greeted them, then motioned for them to sit. He pointed to a box on the corner of his desk that was sealed and marked with his initials.

"RuthAnn's personal effects. What there is of them. She was hysterical at first, mostly from fear. When we got her calmed down enough to be lucid, she agreed to the usual tests, including the rape kit. But as we were finishing up, she became paranoid and frightened again. That's when she asked for the lawyer. One of you will need to sign for the kit," he told Ray and Jeff.

"I will," offered Ray.

Nick nodded, then leaned forward. "Look, I don't know exactly what happened to this woman, but she's been brutalized. She was mumbling when they brought her in, probably from dehydration. No idea how long she'd been in that room alone. We called Legal Aid, and they're going to send someone over."

"Did she say why she wanted a lawyer?" Jeff asked.

Nick shook his head. "She said very little after that."

Lindsey scooted to the edge of her chair. "Have you called her family?"

"She didn't have any numbers with her when they brought her in."

Lindsey nodded. "There should be an address book at her house, and I have her emergency contact information at the restaurant."

Nick turned to Lindsey. "You need to know that whatever is going on with her, some of it is aimed at you. She kept repeating, 'Tell Lindsey. Tell Lindsey.'"

"Tell me what?"

Nick shrugged. "She never got that part out. We hoped with you here, she might calm down, give us some idea about what happened."

A tap on the door was followed by a nurse, who looked pointedly at Nick. He nodded at her and she left.

"I've got to get back out on the floor. We admitted RuthAnn. Wait here, and I'll have one of the orderlies escort you to her room."

Fifteen minutes later, Ray was on his way to the Skyliner, while Lindsey and Jeff sat in a semidark hospital room, watching a sleeping RuthAnn breathe.

"I was just here," muttered Jeff.

"Beg pardon?"

"I've spent more time in the hospital in the past week than I have since I was a kid."

"That's what you get for hanging out with me."

"Well, I knew being around you was exciting. Never occurred to me it was dangerous, too."

"Life's never dull when you're with a Presley girl."

"So Ray and Daniel keep telling me."

"So do you think you'd like it?" Lindsey chewed her lower lip, as surprised by the question as Jeff seemed to be.

He took a long time to answer, and Lindsey wondered if she'd gone too far. It wasn't as if they'd dated. It was just…the more she was around Jeff, the more she wanted to be.

"Yeah," he said slowly. "I think I'd like it a lot."

RuthAnn moaned and twisted in her bed, and both of them stood, waiting to see if she'd wake up. She didn't at first. Instead, she continued to twist, mumbling just beneath her breath, as if she were fighting the sedation. Lindsey moved closer, watching the woman she'd worked with, a woman she thought of as a friend. Even in the dim light of the room, many of RuthAnn's injuries made Lindsey wince in sympathy.

Bruises and cuts covered the left side of RuthAnn's face. Abrasions and puckered burns ran up and down both arms, and deep, purple ligature marks circled both wrists and her throat.

"What happened to you?" Lindsey whispered. She turned to Jeff behind her. "Do you think Todd Lawson did this?"

He didn't answer at first, as if he didn't want to. Then he said simply, "Yes."

"We have to stop him."

"We will."

An hour later, they still sat, observing Ruth-Ann, when Deb, the nurse who had cared for Jeff the night before, came in to check RuthAnn's vitals. She did a double take when she saw Jeff.

"Well, you look better than the last time I saw you."

"Thanks."

Deb completed her tasks as routinely as usual, then left. Half an hour later, a bedraggled young man in a crumpled suit entered, looking inquisitively at Jeff and Lindsey, then RuthAnn.

"RuthAnn Crenshaw?"

Jeff pointed at the bed.

The man let out a very long, exhausted sigh. "They said she asked for a lawyer."

"Before they sedated her," Lindsey explained.

"Great. How long has she been out?"

Jeff checked his watch. "More than ninety minutes."

"And you are…?"

"Jeffrey Gage. I'm with the Bell County Sheriff's Department."

Lindsey also stepped forward and introduced herself. "RuthAnn works for me," she explained.

The man shook their hands. "Mr. Harper, with Legal Aid." He gave Jeff a confused look. "You said you're from Bell County. I was told Ms. Crenshaw was found at the Skyliner. That's Robertson County."

"We think what happened to her is part of an ongoing investigation in Bell County," Jeff explained.

"I see. Are you here to arrest her?"

Jeff shook his head. "Just talk."

The young man brushed his hair off his forehead, then reached in his pocket for a business card. "Well, no talking without me present. Understand?"

Jeff took the card. "I won't ask her a thing."

"Good. I've got two other clients I'm going to check on, then I'll be back."

"Did you draw the short straw tonight down at Legal Aid?" Jeff asked.

A grin crossed Harper's face, then vanished. "Later." He left, only to return a few minutes later, addressing Jeff. "Cute answer, by the way. Let me be clear. Don't ask, don't tell, don't say a word to her and if she tries to talk, tell her I'll be right back. Got it?"

Jeff nodded.

Lindsey stood beside him as Harper left again. "What was that all about?"

"Precision. Lawyers are trained how to use it for their clients and against the system. When I said I wouldn't ask RuthAnn anything, what I did *not* say was that I wouldn't talk to her. He recognized the difference and called me on it. If he hadn't, I would have, in fact, talked to her. He's good. He'll do well by her."

"Do all lawyers think like that?"

"Yep. They're trained to."

Lindsey still couldn't understand why Ruth-Ann needed a lawyer in the first place. She was getting tired of waiting for her coworker to wake up so she could find out. "You want some coffee?" she asked Jeff.

"Absolutely. I'll get it. Will do me good to stretch my legs some."

Lindsey watched him go, marveling at his patience. He seemed to be content to watch RuthAnn sleep, standing over her, occasionally having these bits of conversation. Ever since they'd entered the room, she'd fought the urge to shake RuthAnn awake and demand to know what was going on. They'd made such progress today, pinning down that this was about Todd Lawson, even discovering that the boy in the coma may be Todd's son.

It was as if, for the first time since this started, they had a direction, some idea of what might be going on, instead of random bits of information that led nowhere. But now this development with RuthAnn… It made no sense in the scenario they'd painted today. Lindsey wanted to call Ray, hear what he found at the motel. Anything!

She walked to the window and peered out. While they'd been watching RuthAnn, darkness had covered Springfield. House lights and streetlights had popped on, dotting the landscape like fallen stars. It was beautiful, but all Lindsey could see was that they had wasted time, with nothing accomplished.

"Lindsey?" The word was a barely audible croak.

She whirled. RuthAnn's eyes were open, but she blinked, then rubbed at them, as if trying to clear away a fog.

Lindsey went to the bedside. "I'm here. How do you feel?"

"Awful. Did they call a lawyer?" RuthAnn swallowed hard and licked her lips.

Lindsey filled a cup with water from a pitcher on the lift table. "Yes. He's been in. A Mr. Harper. He'll be back in a few minutes."

RuthAnn pushed up on one elbow and took the water, sipping slowly. "I should wait for him."

"RuthAnn, why do you need a lawyer? You were attacked. You didn't do anything wrong."

RuthAnn sipped again. "You really have no idea, do you?"

"I know Todd Lawson probably did this to you."

RuthAnn's hands began to shake, sloshing some of the water out. Lindsey took the cup and set it aside, then helped RuthAnn lean back.

"I'll get the nurse."

RuthAnn's thin hand clutched Lindsey's blouse. "You're next, you know. He said to tell you that you were next. That he'd finish what he started. You're next."

FOURTEEN

As Lindsey and Jeff waited in the hall for Mr. Harper to finish interviewing RuthAnn, she filled him in on her conversation with RuthAnn. He listened carefully, tamping down the emotions her words stirred in him, especially the desire to close his hands around Todd Lawson's throat. "Do you know what he means—'finish what he started'?"

Lindsey shook her head. "I just took it to mean that he planned to kill me. But we already knew that. I'm already looking around every bush and behind every tree, thinking he'll be there. I don't know how I could be more scared, although I know I would be if you weren't here."

Jeff started to respond, to promise to stay with her, but the door to RuthAnn's room opened, and Harper emerged, looking more exhausted than ever. Dark circles blotted the skin under his eyes. He looked from one to the other, then licked his lips before speaking.

"She definitely needs a lawyer—" he held up a hand to keep Lindsey from interrupting "—and that's all I'm going to say." He looked at Jeff. "You're not going to arrest her?"

"Not without evidence that she's committed a crime. We'd want to hold her as a material witness, but I can't imagine she's going anywhere right now."

"No, and you won't be able to question her tonight. She's already asleep again. They'll probably release her tomorrow. Despite how nasty her injuries are, none are life-threatening. As soon as they're satisfied that there's no internal bleeding or that she's not a danger to herself, they'll let her go."

"That soon? I heard she was ranting up a storm when she came in," Jeff said calmly.

Harper didn't respond at first, just shifted his briefcase from one hand to the other. "I'll pick her up when they release her. I'm going to arrange a spot for her in a safe house I know."

Jeff thought about that for a moment. "You think she needs a security guard tonight?"

"Probably a good idea."

"She's afraid he'll come here?"

"Terrified. And after what they did to her, I can't blame her. All her injuries? They were done *for fun*."

Jeff nodded. "Got it. I'll make it happen."

"Thanks."

"We'll talk tomorrow."

"No doubt." Harper walked off, glancing back at Jeff once. Jeff acknowledged the clear message that the young lawyer had given him. He crushed his coffee cup, then looked down at Lindsey. "We've got a problem."

"Besides the fact that I'm being stalked by a man who hurts women for fun?"

Jeff took her arm and pulled her toward the end of the hall as he took out his cell phone. "Harper said, 'after what *they* did to her.' That was intentional."

Lindsey's breath caught in her throat. "Todd Lawson isn't working alone."

"No, and that's the missing piece of the puzzle." Jeff hit a speed-dial number on his phone. "We've been wondering how Lawson found you after all these years. It had to be through someone here in Bell County. Someone who knows you both. And my guess is that RuthAnn has been feeding that person information about you. Maybe even unintentionally. That's why she needs a lawyer. She may have inadvertently set all this in motion, which is why they had to get her out of the picture." His call connected, and Jeff filled Ray in on what they'd learned.

"Good. We can start working that tomorrow. It's after midnight. Take Lindsey home, and y'all get some rest," the sheriff told him. "I talked to the warden up at Riverbend. You have an appointment with Luke Presley at one-thirty tomorrow afternoon."

They left the hospital and headed back to April's. Exhausted, they rode in silence for a while, but Jeff knew he had to let her know about the prison visit. He knew of no other way to break it to her but by blurting it out.

"Ray got me an appointment tomorrow at Riverbend."

After a moment, she whispered, "Okay."

"You want to go?"

She shook her head.

"Anything I should know?"

"I don't know him, Jeff. I haven't seen him since I was eleven. My memories of him are brutal and incomprehensible. They're just blurs of violence that I don't understand."

More miles of silence passed. "Do you remember your dad?" she asked.

Jeff shrugged. "A few things. We have all these pictures of us that help me connect some fleeting memories with events. But the image of him in my head is from the pictures. I don't know if I remember him at all."

"So we have that in common."

"Among other things."

They rode in silence a bit more, then Jeff felt her hand brush his shoulder. Just a touch, but he thought he'd burst with pride. *Lord,* he thought, *help us get through this...and put it all in the past.*

The next morning, Aunt Suke insisted that Lindsey spend the morning baking with her. "You need a break from all this, girl." For once, Lindsey agreed. Around lunchtime, Jeff came by to fill her in on his way out to Riverbend.

"I finished calling all the auto dealers."

"And?"

He shook his head. "Two more dead ends. But a couple sounded promising and said they'd call back. Suspicious folks. I should have let Troy call them. They're probably checking my credentials."

"Which are, of course, impeccable."

Jeff laughed, which she hadn't heard him do in a long time.

"I like it when you laugh."

"Someday, we'll both do a lot more of it."

"Promise?"

"Absolutely." He paused, then stroked her face,

a gesture that made her want to be with him that much more.

Lindsey watched Jeff drive away, almost wishing she had the fortitude to go with him, to look her father in the face once again. To show him that he hadn't defeated her or any of them. *No matter what you did, we succeeded.*

And they had. She smiled, thinking about the lives her sisters had now, despite the horrible circumstances they'd endured. Mama had been right. *Jehovah-jireh.* God who provides.

Lindsey closed the heavy wooden front door when Jeff left and leaned against it, relishing the warmth of the house. The scent of cinnamon and brown sugar permeated the house, a result of Aunt Suke's early morning baking. A softly crackling fire burned in the parlor fireplace, adding a calming mood to the room. Christmas and Thanksgiving decorations spilled out of a box nearby, and Lindsey knew Aunt Suke was keeping her promise about decorating the entire house for the holidays. Gentle voices drifted down to her from upstairs, the firm voice of Aunt Suke and the protesting one of Daniel, who had made it quite plain that he didn't want to decorate for Christmas until after Thanksgiving. Then, April's sweet alto, trying to placate them both.

Lindsey almost wished she could stay here

through Christmas, to see what Daniel, April and Aunt Suke came up with, but she knew that wouldn't happen. After this was over, Lindsey wanted to go back to her little house in town. Maybe put up her own tree. Because now she realized it wasn't *this* house she wanted. For the first time in her life, she wanted a real home of her own.

A quiet knock on the front door shook her out of her reverie. She pulled it open, grinning when she saw who stood there. "Hey, there! I was just thinking that I needed to call you. Come on in."

She turned to lead her guest inside, only to have a sudden explosion of pain shoot through her skull, throwing her world into darkness.

Riverbend Maximum Security Institution, as the name implied, sat in one of the gentle bends of the Cumberland River. It was built to replace the Tennessee State Penitentiary, a legendary gothic structure that looked more like a medieval castle than a prison. "The Castle" drew photographers from around the world and was often used as a movie set.

Riverbend, however, was nowhere near as romantic as its predecessor. It was low, blocky, functional and well run—just as a prison should be. Jeff had visited several times in the past, a loathsome part of his job. He knew how grim a Riverbend life had to be.

And when the guards escorted Luke Presley into the visitors' area, Jeff could see the result of a harsh prison existence. At fifty-one, Luke Presley had the haggard, deeply creviced face of a man in his seventies. His gray, blotchy skin emphasized the dullness in his eyes. *Prison life,* thought Jeff. His hands and feet still shackled, Luke shuffled comfortably over to the waiting chair, obviously familiar with moving around in the chains. He dropped into the chair, carefully eyeing Jeff's uniform. When he spoke, Luke's voice had the familiar gravel of vocal cords long damaged by smoke and booze, but his tone held a surprising calmness.

"Sheriff's deputy. But I don't know you."

"I'm Jeff Gage, and I'm a deputy with the Bell County Sheriff's Department."

A light of recognition shone in Luke's eyes. "Bell County, huh? I hear odd things are going on up there."

"What have you heard?"

Luke smiled, but it was an expression coated in sadness, not joy. "My attorney tells me that my daughters have settled up there. Is that true?"

Jeff studied the older man's face, trying to get

a read on some kind of emotion, but Luke's face showed little. "It is."

"Are they doing well?"

Jeff hadn't planned to tell Luke anything about his daughters, but he hadn't expected the questions, either. "Two of them are. But your youngest has had something out of your past come back to endanger her."

"July?"

"Yes."

"What's going on?"

"I need to hear your version of what happened the day Karen Lawson died."

Luke sat still for a long time. Then he shifted in his chair. "Todd Lawson has finally found her?"

Jeff stiffened. "You knew?"

Luke rolled his shoulders and sat back in the chair. "I knew he'd be looking for July Presley. We didn't think he'd ever find Lindsey Purvis."

The pieces began to fall into place for Jeff. "You're the one who got her name changed?"

Luke shrugged. "The criminal courts wouldn't believe me, but the Family Court finally got the message when Todd attacked my mother-in-law one day. July never realized why she couldn't stay with her grandmother anymore, why she had to go into foster care. We thought July had pretty much blocked out the day Karen died."

"She has."

"Good."

"Why didn't you ever tell the cops you were sleeping with Karen Lawson?"

Luke gave a harsh bark of a laugh. "Because Todd had tried to kill my daughter and me, and almost succeeded. He told me that if I said a word, he'd make sure none of us left the house again, and I'd be blamed for it all. The man is a sadist, and I believed every word he said." He motioned around the room. "I kept my mouth shut, but it didn't help. Looks like he got his way no matter what."

"What happened that day?"

Luke clutched his hands together, bracing them on the table. "Karen always picked up Sasha and July from school, then drove over and picked up the boys and brought them all home. July played there with Sasha until Evie or I got home. That's how I met Karen. Anyway, that day, I get off work early, so I decide to get July ahead of schedule. Maybe spend more time with Karen.

"Anyway, I see their car in the driveway, the trunk lid up, and I pull in behind it. All of a sudden Todd comes barreling out of the garage, swinging this switchblade he always carried, and lights into me. Calls me names. I dodged the knife, but he whacked me around pretty good. Next thing I know, July's on his back, screaming bloody murder. He grabs her by the hair and pulls her off, which gives me a chance to get the knife. He doesn't even slow down. Knocks July out with his fist, then threatens me."

"So you go get drunk?"

Luke didn't say anything for a few moments. "Yeah. I'm sure the girls have told you I wasn't much of a man in those days."

"Something like that."

"Believe 'em. I'm not that man now, but I sure was then. Anyway, I wake up and Karen is gone and July's out of her head scared to death. Won't let anyone touch her but her mama. Screams bloody murder if anyone else even tries. We sent her to her grandmother's."

He straightened. "Then all of a sudden there's Todd Lawson, all over the television, acting like a pure fool who don't know nothing. All innocent. Right." He ran his hands through his hair. "He's why I'm in here."

He paused, eyed Jeff. "Is it true that he's down in Mexico somewhere, hiding out? Scot-free?"

Jeff nodded. "Most of the time."

"Figures. Lawyers. They never get what's coming to 'em." He stopped. "What do you mean, most of the time?"

"We think he's in Bell County right now. Trying to kill Lin—July. Again."

Luke flared. "That rotten—!"

"You want payback?"

Luke stilled. "What?"

"Tell me something that could put him away."

Luke paused. "You got something to record this with?"

Lindsey hurt. All of her—her head most of all. She tried to open her eyes, but even the dim light around her hurt, and she squeezed them shut again. She lay on a stone floor, her cheek pressed against it. The chilly air around her held the aromas of cooking oil, cinnamon and rosemary. Cold seeped through every joint. Her arms were wrenched behind her, making her shoulders shriek with pain. Her hands were tied together. So were her knees and ankles. She tried to move, but moaned instead.

"Ah, our princess awakens."

The voice from the wreck. The voice that had taunted her at the house.

Todd Lawson. Where…?

The voice hovered over her, growing closer with each word. "Do you have any idea, princess, what it's like to plan not only the perfect crime, but the perfect *murder,* only to have it destroyed, *ruined,* by an eleven-year-old snoop and her drunken slob of a father? The snoop who saw all the things she shouldn't have seen, that no one should have seen?"

A hand grabbed a chunk of her hair and yanked her head backward. "Do you?"

Lindsey screamed.

Todd Lawson laughed, a false-sounding bellow, which soon dropped into a throaty chortle that spoke of a lack of sanity. He leaned over, his face close to hers. "Scream, princess. No one can hear. Thanks to you."

Me? Lindsey opened her eyes and looked around. The familiar walls of the restaurant cellar told her exactly what he meant. The building sat back from the road. Closed up tight. By her choice.

"I couldn't believe how easy you were to manipulate. You and Deputy Dawg, running around like chickens with a fox in the henhouse. One push, and you focus on RuthAnn. Another push, you move out of your house. Yet another, and you close this place up. In less than a week, I knew where you were going to be every minute of the day. I couldn't believe you were that stupid."

"But why? I don't even remember anything about that day!"

Todd mocked her. "You don't remember? Poor baby. Guess what?" He bent over her face again. "I don't care! You ruined my life! You saw everything, and your dad showed up where he was never supposed to be. I knew I could keep him quiet, but I knew you'd squawk to your mother. I'd have to take care of both of you. Did her, but you'd already disappeared."

Lindsey stared at him. "You killed my mother? But my father—"

"Wasn't as lucky."

Todd grabbed her and set her upright, her back against a support post. He looped a leather strap around her neck, binding her to the post and almost cutting off her air. He then grabbed the sleeves of her shirt and ripped them down from the shoulder seams, exposing her biceps.

She could still scream. Someone might hear. Maybe a customer? Then her heart sank, and her shoulders slumped. No, the closest business to her would be…

"Max," she whispered.

It all fell into place now, and an ache of betrayal and fury shot through her. Max had been the one who had befriended RuthAnn and gotten information about her new boss. "Lindsey

Presley, aka Lindsey Purvis, née July Presley."
Max had fed it to Todd Lawson and lured him
back to Tennessee.

And it was Max who had stood at the front
door of Daniel and April's home, coming in
friendship, just to collect the rent. Such a friend
that Lindsey had turned her back…

"Old Maxie's not here right now. But he will
be. I've given him a lot of grief about you, and
he definitely wants a chance at you. You ruined
his life, as well."

"How?"

"Just by showing up, little girl. Just by showing up. Y'see, Max had the unfortunate luck to
have married my sister. I've had him looking for
you for years. Then you just moved in right next
door. He wasn't sure at first, then you admitted
to RuthAnn you'd changed your name."

Lindsey shuddered, both from cold and dread.
"You tortured RuthAnn."

"And enjoyed every minute of it. At first, it
was just to get more details about you. Then,
after that…" He shrugged, then grinned. "After
that it was just for fun. Couldn't let her scream,
though, because of where we were. You, though.
I want you to scream." Todd reached into his
pants pockes and pulled out a pack of cigarettes
and a lighter.

Lindsey gasped, remembering the round, puckered burns up and down RuthAnn's arms. "No!"

Todd Lawson grinned and lit the cigarette.

FIFTEEN

Jeff played the recording in Ray's office, watching as the sheriff's face alternately flushed and paled as he listened. Jeff knew his own blood ran cold every time he listened to it. When it finished, Jeff turned off the recorder.

Ray looked at him, his face drawn tight. "Do you believe him?"

"I do. I don't think he would have made up the specific details about how Karen was hogtied in the trunk of the car or the way her arm had been broken. I called Mark Bradley back, and he confirmed that Karen's skeletal remains revealed that exact break."

Ray looked away into some far distance, his eyes glassy. "You almost hope Lindsey never remembers."

Jeff tucked the recording in his pocket. "In fact, I pray she doesn't. And there may be a way we don't have to ask her to."

"I'm listening."

"Lawson's been investigating her enough to know she hasn't talked yet. He may even know she has no memory of that day. But he needs to kill her, just in case she ever does remember. What would happen if he thinks she's about to tell us, officially?"

"A deposition."

"We could play this—"

A tap on Ray's door interrupted Jeff, and one of the other deputies stuck his head in. "Sorry. Jeff, you have a call. Said he was some auto shop in Kansas, returning your call."

"I'll get it." He went back to his desk and grabbed the phone. "This is Jeff Gage."

"Yeah, you'd called about a part I sold for a 1968 GTO."

"I appreciate you calling back. The car is in our impound lot and we're trying to track down the owner. The title was a bust, so we're tracing the replacement parts."

"Gotcha. Have the invoice right here. It went to a mailbox drop."

The dealer read the address, and Jeff wrote it down slowly, staring at the words in disbelief. He asked the man to repeat it. Nothing had changed. He had heard it right the first time. When he looked up, Ray stood by his desk.

"You're white as a sheet. What did you find out?"

Jeff handed him the slip of paper. "The part was shipped to this address."

Ray read it and looked at Jeff. "Get your kit."

"Ray!"

They looked at the dispatcher, who stood in the door of her office, the phone cord dangling from one ear.

"Daniel just called in on the 911 line. Lindsey's missing. They can't find her anywhere."

Ray and Jeff looked at each other, then down at the paper in Ray's hand.

"It has to be," Jeff said, fear coursing through every vein. "Has to be."

Ray turned around and called each of the five deputies in the bullpen by name. "Take your vests." He recited the address. "We're going. Now!"

Jeff grabbed his kit. "I'll call the judge on the way for the warrant."

Searing pain radiated from the first cigarette burn through Lindsey's biceps, spearing into her brain. Her head fell forward, and she tried to draw her knees up, to brace herself against the post. It might help. Maybe. Or not.

Her mind flew backward in time, to her childhood, to those moments when her father's rage had exploded with flying fists. How she had dealt with the pain. Most of all, her mind went to a time when her mother had calmed him down. She'd distracted him from the violence with questions that seemed to come from nowhere. Anything to direct his attention away from the girls.

"I thought you would have screamed more." Todd squatted in front of her. "Perhaps I didn't hold it against your skin long enough." He reached out and stroked Lindsey's cheek with the back of his hand, then tucked his hand under her chin and lifted her head. "Or perhaps I chose the wrong area of your body. Some places are naturally more tender than others."

"Why the GTO?"

Todd blinked. "What?"

Lindsey swallowed hard and tried to speak firmly, evenly. "Why did you choose the GTO? Why send your son in the GTO?"

Todd stood, his face showing genuine surprise. "You're serious. You really don't know about the car."

Lindsey shook her head.

Todd stared at her. "I thought you were lying. You really don't remember what happened that day, do you? All this, and you don't even remember." He lay his cigarette on a shelf behind him, and took a swig of water from a bottle on the same shelf.

Lindsey shook her head and drew her knees even tighter to her chest, waiting, glancing up at the set of shelves behind Todd.

It might work. Maybe. Eventually, he would come closer again.

Todd coughed, then took another swig. "It was a GTO you escaped from, darling. A GTO that had Karen in the trunk. I called her, told her to meet me at the house. Wanted to pick up the boys together for a family dinner before she went to work. But I was waiting. I got her and Sasha in the trunk, but you got away from me. If your old man hadn't showed up, I would have found you, too. I locked you in there with her and Sasha, but, no, you had to shove the backseat out enough to wriggle through. I wanted to remind you of our time together once before. It's why I threw in the book and the knife, as well."

Lindsey scowled. "What knife?"

Todd grinned. "What? Your precious sheriff's deputy didn't tell you about the knife?"

"What knife?" she repeated.

He leered at her. "The one that killed Karen. It cut your father, too, for sticking his nose in where it didn't belong." He squatted in front of her. "But all for naught, as it turns out. I had planned such a delicious show for your murder, but you ruined it all."

Come closer, Todd. Closer. "Too bad you wasted a magnificent machine on someone who couldn't appreciate your choice. You restored it yourself, didn't you?"

Todd's mouth twisted. "Flattery will not distract me, my dear." He sighed. "But it was a beautiful car."

"Did you buy it local?"

"A salvage yard in Kentucky." Todd's eyes narrowed.

"Where did you get the replacement parts?"

"Different dealers." He moved closer, trailing one finger along the outside of her thigh, and every muscle tensed. "Why all this curiosity about a car you don't even remember?" He reached for her face.

Bracing her back against the post, Lindsey lashed out with her feet, planting both heels in Todd's solar plexus and shoving with all her strength. His breath rushed out of him with a harsh whoosh, and he stumbled backward, completely off balance. He fell into the shelves behind him hard. They rocked backward, and Todd's cigarette and water tipped to the floor. As Todd scrambled to recover, the shelves rocked forward, dislodging everything on the top four shelves. Pans rained down on him, and Lindsey watched in anticipation as a five-gallon tin of cooking oil on the top shelf tottered...rocked... and fell, striking Todd in the head before crashing to the floor.

Todd dropped, unconscious.

Lindsey knew he wouldn't be out long. She struggled and tried to push herself up. If she could stand, she might find a way to loosen her bonds...

Then she froze. The drop to the floor had cracked the tin. Cooking oil oozed out, soaking Todd's pants, and edging ever closer to his still-lit cigarette.

Four patrol cars converged on Maxwell Carpenter's courier business, the address the Kansas auto dealer had given Jeff. Two of them blocked the main highway in front of it, while the two others pulled into the driveway. As officers surrounded the house, Ray and Jeff approached the front door of the small building, cautiously, each standing to one side.

Ray knocked, then shouted. "Max! It's Ray Taylor! You need to come out here! Open the door slowly!"

After a few moments, they heard the lock

snap. The door cracked open, and Max peered out. "I'm not armed!"

"Then step out here. Hands raised. Let us see them."

The door opened wider, and Max, looking smaller and weaker than ever, appeared, his hands over his head. Jeff grabbed him and pulled him out on the porch. He cuffed Max's wrists, then patted him down.

Max protested. "I'm not armed! I told you. I didn't touch her. I never touched her! I never touched either of them!"

Jeff shoved Max down the steps toward another officer. "Watch him."

Ray and Jeff entered the building, well aware that Todd Lawson was far more dangerous than Max. Two other officers followed. The courier business was small, consisting only of an office, a reception space with a rack of mailboxes and four rooms of storage. No basement.

No Lindsey.

Frustrated, they returned to the porch. Ray holstered his gun. "I'll call the judge, see if we can get a warrant for his house—"

A twitchy movement from Max caught Jeff's eye, and he motioned Ray to stop for a moment.

"What's going on?"

"Max is acting odd." Jeff moved a bit to his

right, so that he could watch Max, but he was blocked from Max's sight by Ray.

"Max always acts odd. What's he doing?"

"He's… Okay, that's three times he's looked over at the restaurant."

Ray nodded. "Let's go." He motioned for two officers to follow them, and they headed for the back of the café.

As they closed in, Jeff got a whiff of an acrid scent. "Smoke?"

Ray pointed. "Coming out of the cellar." They broke into a run, and Ray barked at one of the officers, "Call the fire department."

Then tendrils of smoke peeled away from the edges of the cellar doors, but the wood was cool. The locks wouldn't budge, so Ray motioned everyone back as Jeff took aim and fired. The newly installed apparatus shattered, and they yanked open the doors. Grayish-white smoke roiled out, almost blinding them.

"Over here!" Lindsey's voice penetrated the smoke. "Stay low!"

Covering their mouths and crouching, Jeff and Ray entered. They followed Lindsey's calls and coughs 'til they found her, tied and pressed as close to the floor as possible. Nearby, Todd lay unconscious, as flames licked up his right leg and across his stomach. Jeff cut her bonds and scooped her up, holding her tight to his chest as Ray grabbed Todd under the arms and dragged him out.

Outside, they all fell to the ground. Another officer used a blanket to extinguish the flames on Todd Lawson.

Lindsey clung to Jeff, weeping and coughing. The smoke inhalation had almost overcome her. Jeff thought his heart would break as he pulled her into his lap and held her close. *Please, Lord, let this be over.*

As the sirens of the fire trucks and ambulances closed in, Jeff and Lindsey watched tendrils of flame lick up and out of the cellar, crossing over the wall and attacking the roof. The firefighters tried, but the battle had already been lost. Slowly, Lindsey's dream was consumed by fire.

SIXTEEN

A few hours later, Jeff sat by Lindsey's hospital bed, watching her breathe. Smoke inhalation could be tricky, lingering long after the fire. They had been walking away from the restaurant when Lindsey had collapsed against him, coughing uncontrollably. The EMTs grabbed her and headed for NorthCrest, one more time. She slept now, the oxygen cannula still in place. Behind him, June, Daniel and April waited, as well, each of them lost in their own thoughts.

She almost died.

Jeff couldn't dispel the thought. It clung to him, swirling over and over in his head. As clumsy as his investigation had been in the beginning, toward the end, Jeff recognized that his insights, his hunches, had come through. They had succeeded, and the bad guys had been brought down.

Yet he felt nothing like a hero.

She almost died.

The soft whisper of the door behind him told

Jeff that Ray had returned. They all looked expectantly at him, and he shook his head. "Todd Lawson never regained consciousness. He died about ten minutes ago."

Bad guy vanquished. But there was no satisfaction in it. No sense of justice. Karen and Sasha Lawson were still in their graves, Luke Presley still sat in prison and a childhood trauma long forgotten would now haunt Lindsey the rest of her life.

She almost died.

Jeff felt Ray move in behind him. "How is she?"

"She almost died."

Ray remained silent a few moments. "But she didn't. And she won't. And you have the chance to make it right."

"I don't deserve her."

"Who really deserves the people we love? They're God's gifts. Not because *we're* all that. Because *He* is."

It was as much, if not more, than Jeff had ever heard Ray say about his faith.

Yet it was enough.

He'd make it right.

Lindsey awoke to excited whispers. She swallowed hard and licked her lips. "What's going on?"

The whispers turned to cries of glee as her family swarmed around her bed. Lindsey jerked back against her pillow at the sudden rush of bodies.

"'Bout time you woke up," June said, barely containing her joy.

April nudged Jeff. "Go on. Show her."

He scowled at both of them. "She just woke up."

"She's a girl," April protested. "She won't care."

"She's in the hospital. I wouldn't count on that. I had also planned to do it privately."

June stared at him, incredulous. "Have you learned nothing about this family?"

"Water, please," Lindsey croaked. "Y'know, for the *patient* in the room?"

June beat Jeff to the cup, but he helped her sit up as June held the water. Lindsey drank greedily, then pushed it aside and cleared her throat. She looked up at Jeff and smiled sweetly. "Whatever it is, you might as well do it now." She raised the head of the bed some and pushed herself up. "Do I need to guess? Flowers? Balloons?"

Jeff flushed, then slowly held out an envelope. Curious, Lindsey reached for it and lifted the flap. Inside was a check. When she looked at the amount, the breath stopped in her chest, and she coughed. She looked from it to Jeff and back to the check.

"I know you had insurance, but," he began.

"Jeff did that," interrupted June. "He's been all over Bell County the past couple of days, telling people what this county and the restaurant mean to you. What you can do for the county by being a success."

"I just explained—"

April continued. "He set up the donation account at the bank. That's just the first installment. Money's still coming in."

Lindsey stared at him, even though tears blinded her. "I thought it was all gone."

"So you'll want to rebuild here?" he asked. "The folks here really want you to."

She nodded furiously. "Of course, I do."

"Alan and I can help you rebuild—" Jeff's words broke off when June nudged him. He stepped closer to the bed. "But, actually, I was hoping we could build more than a new restaurant."

Her eyes narrowed in curiosity. "Like what?"

"A family."

This time, Jeff's hand held a small box, which he opened slowly. The diamond ring inside glistened. "I know this may not be the right time, but—"

"It is," she said, her voiced cracking. She swallowed, asking God for the right words. "Jeff, I know better than anyone that life is short and can be rough. I thought I was okay going through it alone, just me and my dreams. But the past few days have shown me that I'm not. I need my sisters. And I need you. I love you."

Jeff's face flushed as he fumbled the ring out of the box.

"Don't drop it," Ray commanded.

Lindsey grinned and held up her left hand. Jeff slipped the ring on it. "Then will you marry me?"

She nodded. "Absolutely."

EPILOGUE

Evelyn May cooed, a sweet, wet sound that turned Lindsey to mush. She pulled the baby carrier a little closer, careful not to disturb either the six-tiered cake or the emerald green-and-silver decorations April and June had spent the night draping all over the dining room of the new restaurant.

Lindsey inhaled deeply. Everything still smelled so new, like freshly sawn wood and paint. All the inspections had been done, and she'd passed with flying colors. Employees had been hired and foodstuffs unpacked and stored. She hadn't baked so much as a cookie, but already the sweet scent of cinnamon lingered in the air.

And it really belongs to all of us—everyone in town. The thought made Lindsey want to burst from pure joy. The rebuilding process had indeed been a community affair. The people who'd donated money felt a sense of ownership, and many had turned out to pound nails, paint a wall or unpack food. Alan and Jeff had done a lot of the work, as well, working here whenever they could, turning it into a second home.

In fact, Jeff had been on his back, under the sink, adjusting a fitting on her grease trap, when he suggested that they marry here. She'd laughed, then realized he was serious. "It would be like a grand opening, only you wouldn't have to cook."

Well, almost. Lindsey looked up again at the green-and-white cake, topped by a green-and-silver starburst. *I did make the cake.*

Evie fussed again.

"Oh, all right," Lindsey whispered. "Just one more. But don't tell your mama." She ran her finger along the backside of the cake, where no one would see, scraping up a morsel of green icing. She held it to her niece's mouth, and Evie sucked hungrily on it.

"Don't you be giving my baby sugar!" April scolded. She and June had entered from the kitchen, their matching green bridesmaid's dresses rustling as they strode across the room.

Lindsey grinned. "Would I do that?"

"Of course, you would!" April bent, peering into Evie's carrier. "Plus, there's evidence all around her mouth."

Lindsey shook a finger at the baby. "I told you not to tell on me."

With an expertise that only seemed to come with motherhood, April whisked a wet wipe out of the diaper bag and cleaned Evie's face. Then she gave Lindsey a quick kiss on the cheek. "You look beautiful. I'm going to take her out to Aunt Suke. Be right back." She hefted the carrier and headed back through the kitchen.

June grinned at her baby sister. "Come on. Stand up. Turn around. Let me see."

Lindsey held her arms out and turned around slowly, as June checked her over, smoothing out the skirt of her tea-length gown and straightening the lace on her shoulders. She ran her hands up and down Lindsey's arms, smoothing the lace gloves that stretched up over her elbow.

"Good, good. No slip showing, everything's lined up." She plucked an imaginary loose thread from Lindsey's arm. "Now. Count them off. Something old?"

"The ribbons in my hair are from Aunt Suke's debutante bouquet."

"Something new?"

Lindsey waggled her left hand, where her engagement ring sparkled.

"Something borrowed?"

"Your wedding shoes."

"Something blue?"

"The garter."

"Then it looks like you're ready to get married."

Lindsey gave June a quick hug. "Thank you. For everything."

"I think this was more God's arranging than mine."

"Still. You were listening."

June looked her sister over, curiosity in her eyes. "You're tense. Are you scared?"

Lindsey rocked up on her toes. "Does it show that much? I wouldn't want Jeff to think that—"

June laughed. "Girl, are you kidding me? That boy's petrified. I think he must have drunk a gallon of water this morning, trying to keep his mouth from drying out."

Lindsey hesitated, a moment of panic tightening her stomach. "You don't think he wants to back out, do you?"

June shook her head. "No, silly. What I'm saying is that you're both scared, and you should be. Marriage isn't an easy thing to take on. It's a lot harder than, say, opening a restaurant. Or even rebuilding a restaurant."

Lindsey smiled, looking around the dining room of the reborn Coffee-Time Café. The newly constructed building had been modeled on the style and atmosphere of the original, but everything in it was brand-new and up-to-date. The dining room, decorated in white linen, green silk and silver lace for their reception, looked like a fairy-tale setting. And she could think of no better way to reopen it than by letting both of her dreams come true at the same time.

June patted her arm again. "I'll go get Ray. You take a few deep breaths."

As the door closed behind June, Lindsey pulled one of the chairs out and sat. Her bouquet—white roses and dark green satin ribbon—lay on the table. A slip of paper peeked out from between two of the flowers, and she frowned at it.

"Here, now," she whispered. "You're not supposed to be showing." She pulled it free. "My real 'something new.'" Lindsey unfolded the note, which had arrived only yesterday, reading it for the umpteenth time.

Lindsey (although I will always think of you as July),
Your letters finally got through to this stubborn old man. I just never believed you'd want to hear from me again, after all I did. But I guess you're as stubborn as I am. I am eternally grateful for the efforts you've

*made on my behalf. Although Lawson's con-
fession to you isn't enough to get me out, I'm
thankful that you know, and that you cared
enough to ask Mr. Harper for help. He's a
good man, a good lawyer.*

*A thousand "I'm sorry"s could never
make up for the pain I've inflicted on you
and your sisters. Although I have thrown
myself at God's feet and He has forgiven
me, forgiving myself is the longer journey.
And I never expected you or your sisters
to do so.*

*What I do hope is that you will accept
that I am a changed man—heart and soul—
and that in the future, I pray you will find
God's true path for your life, and that you
will find a way to heal from the damage I
inflicted.*
May God hold you close,
Your father

Lindsey folded the note and returned it to the
bouquet. "Sometimes, Daddy," she whispered,
"your dreams come true. And, sometimes, what
comes true is the real dream."

Jeff tugged at his tie.
"Leave it alone, boy," Ray growled. "It's fine."

"It feels crooked."

"Well, it's not. Stop fidgeting."

Beside them in the copse of trees outside the restaurant, Daniel coughed. "Like you didn't fidget the day you married June," he told Ray.

"I had a lot more to worry about."

"There's April," Daniel said as he looked at the rows of chairs set up for the ceremony. "I'll go see if they're ready." He headed over to where April was settling the baby carrier into a chair next to Aunt Suke.

"Tell me again this is the right thing to do." Despite Ray's protests, Jeff tugged again at his tie.

Ray faced him. "You love her?"

Jeff swallowed hard. "More than anything."

"Don't want to even think about living without her?"

"Not for a second."

"Then it's the right thing to do." Ray pushed Jeff's hand away from his tie. "Look, marriage is never a cakewalk, but if you can think of nothing sweeter than sitting with her on a porch when you're both eighty, then you'll find a way to make it work."

April motioned for Ray to follow her, and he nodded. "I have to go give away a bride. Meet us there."

Jeff nodded. He looked around at the crowd that had gathered for their wedding and swallowed hard. Raising up the new building for the café had brought a bond to Bell's Springs that it hadn't seen in a long time. It was as if everyone in town wanted to see Lindsey succeed, and now they all turned out to see her get married. The parking lot overflowed with people, and cars lined both sides of the highway as far as he could see. Even after he'd suggested it, Jeff had had doubts about getting married here. Now he knew it was exactly the right choice, not only for them, but for the town.

An arched trellis bursting with white roses had been set up under the trees at the edge of the lot, and the minister waited there, along with a duo of guitarists. Rows of white chairs framed a makeshift aisle from the restaurant's door to the trellis. As the guests found places to stand or sit, two young girls in green silk walked among them, handing out small gauze bags of birdseed to be tossed at the couple after the ceremony.

In the front row of chairs, Aunt Suke made faces at Evie. Aunt Suke's heart tests had been mostly positive, and a stent in one artery had returned her to good health. On the other side of Evie, RuthAnn sat, joining Aunt Suke in the baby play. She still had a haunted look to her eyes, but was well on her way to healing. No charges had been filed against her since she didn't realize her conversations with Max had held such danger. Every so often, Jeff could hear a happy squeal from the baby. Jeff thought about how Daniel and April glowed when talking about their daughter. Their world, their friends seemed back in order.

All of a sudden, he had an image of Lindsey at eighty, her sweet face as lined and soft as Aunt Suke's, with wisdom and love shining in her eyes as she looked at her grandbabies. And at him.

His chest swelled with love. What more could a man ask for?

He headed toward the minister, just as the guitarists began the music, and took his place under the trellis. As they played, Alan emerged from the restaurant with Jeff's mom on one arm. They sat next to Aunt Suke, and his mother winked at him.

Then came the first chords of Pachelbel's *Canon,* which Lindsey had chosen as her processional. Lindsey approached, clinging tight to Ray's arm. Her bouquet, clutched in her right hand, trembled, and Jeff realized she was as scared as he was. But that would work in their favor. Scared would keep them humble, reminding them Who was really the One in control.

As each step brought her closer, sunlight gleamed in her hair, and once again, Jeff imagined her at eighty. "We can do this," he whispered. "It's definitely the right thing to do."

* * * * *

Dear Reader,

I think most of us would like to follow God's chosen path for our lives, even though we may have a little trouble discerning what that path truly looks like. For instance, I've known since I was a child that I would be a writer. But discovering exactly *what* I was supposed to write took a lot longer, mostly because I can be pretty stubborn about trying to follow my dreams instead of God's plan.

In the beginning of this story, Lindsey was just like that. She had her dream of owning her own restaurant, and she was so determined to make it happen that she put people she cared for at risk. Everything changes, however, when she takes Jeff's words to heart: sometimes your dreams come true. And sometimes, what comes true is the real dream. When she let go, the answers began to appear.

I hope you enjoyed reading this book as much as I enjoyed writing it. Here's hoping you get to experience all of God's dreams for you.

Blessings,
Ramona

Questions for Discussion

1. In what ways can you identify with Lindsey? With Jeff?

2. At the heart of the story is Lindsey's determination to succeed after an abusive childhood. Have you or someone you cared about had to heal from a time of violence in their lives?

3. In what ways can forgiveness play a major part in healing from such a trauma?

4. Lindsey moved back to Tennessee to reunite with her sisters and pursue her dream. In what ways do you think this was a wise decision on her part?

5. In the book, there are several references to how different people experience loss and express grief. In what ways have you seen those around you express grief? Have you found it difficult to reach out to people who express loss in unexpected ways?

6. Lindsey uses her grandmother's Bible and her mother's diary as a comforting way to remember her mother and grandmother. In

what ways can small and simple routines in life help us make it through tough times?

7. Other than a death, what events can turn life upside down so that those small routines become vital in making it through? Have there been times when small keepsakes helped you cope with larger trials? Explain.

8. When we look closely at our faith, are there simple and practical elements we can cling to in times of chaos? What are they?

9. Have you ever shared those elements with others who are struggling with difficult events in their lives? Did you see any indications that your faith helped comfort them?

10. Which characters in the book struggle most to remind themselves that God will always protect us from "the snare of the fowler"?

11. What does the restaurant represent for Lindsey, in terms of her dreams of success as well as her battle against her past?

12. In the beginning of the book, do you think Jeff fully understands her determination to keep the restaurant open in the face of the at-

tempts on her life? What makes him finally see what's truly behind her determination?

13. Deciding to close the restaurant represents a major change in Lindsey. What do you think finally brought her to make this decision?

14. As Lindsey struggled to trust God and seek His guidance for her life, she feels God has gone silent. Have you ever felt as if God were letting you down or adding to your problems for some reason? How did you work your way through this?

15. Whose faith do you think is stronger? Which actions in the book reveal the strength of Jeff's and Lindsey's relationships with God?

LARGER-PRINT BOOKS!

**GET 2 FREE
LARGER-PRINT NOVELS
PLUS 2 FREE
MYSTERY GIFTS**

Love Inspired®
SUSPENSE
RIVETING INSPIRATIONAL ROMANCE

Larger-print novels are now available...

YES! Please send me 2 FREE LARGER-PRINT Love Inspired® Suspense novels and my 2 FREE mystery gifts (gifts are worth about $10). After receiving them, if I don't wish to receive any more books, I can return the shipping statement marked "cancel." If I don't cancel, I will receive 4 brand-new novels every month and be billed just $4.99 per book in the U.S. or $5.49 per book in Canada. That's a savings of at least 23% off the cover price. It's quite a bargain! Shipping and handling is just 50¢ per book in the U.S. and 75¢ per book in Canada.* I understand that accepting the 2 free books and gifts places me under no obligation to buy anything. I can always return a shipment and cancel at any time. Even if I never buy another book, the two free books and gifts are mine to keep forever.

110/310 IDN FVZ7

Name _____ (PLEASE PRINT)

Address _____ Apt. #

City _____ State/Prov. _____ Zip/Postal Code

Signature (if under 18, a parent or guardian must sign)

Mail to the Harlequin® Reader Service:
IN U.S.A.: P.O. Box 1867, Buffalo, NY 14240-1867
IN CANADA: P.O. Box 609, Fort Erie, Ontario L2A 5X3

**Are you a current subscriber to Love Inspired Suspense books
and want to receive the larger-print edition?
Call 1-800-873-8635 or visit www.ReaderService.com.**

* Terms and prices subject to change without notice. Prices do not include applicable taxes. Sales tax applicable in N.Y. Canadian residents will be charged applicable taxes. Offer not valid in Quebec. This offer is limited to one order per household. Not valid for current subscribers to Love Inspired Suspense larger print books. All orders subject to credit approval. Credit or debit balances in a customer's account(s) may be offset by any other outstanding balance owed by or to the customer. Please allow 4 to 6 weeks for delivery. Offer available while quantities last.

Your Privacy—The Harlequin® Reader Service is committed to protecting your privacy. Our Privacy Policy is available online at www.ReaderService.com or upon request from the Harlequin Reader Service.

We make a portion of our mailing list available to reputable third parties that offer products we believe may interest you. If you prefer that we not exchange your name with third parties, or if you wish to clarify or modify your communication preferences, please visit us at www.ReaderService.com/consumerschoice or write to us at Harlequin Reader Service Preference Service, P.O. Box 9062, Buffalo, NY 14269. Include your complete name and address.

LISLPDIR13

HEARTWARMING INSPIRATIONAL ROMANCE

Contemporary,
inspirational romances
with Christian characters
facing the challenges
of life and love
in today's world.

**AVAILABLE IN REGULAR
AND LARGER-PRINT FORMATS.**

For exciting stories that reflect traditional values,
visit:
www.ReaderService.com

LIDIR11B

ReaderService.com

Manage your account online!

- Review your order history
- Manage your payments
- Update your address

We've designed the Harlequin® Reader Service website just for you.

Enjoy all the features!

- Reader excerpts from any series
- Respond to mailings and special monthly offers
- Discover new series available to you
- Browse the Bonus Bucks catalog
- Share your feedback

Visit us at:

ReaderService.com

RS13